The Perfect Game

Arlington Aces, Book 3

ELLEY ARDEN

Crimson Romance
New York London Toronto Sydney New Delhi

CRIMSON
ROMANCE

Crimson Romance
An Imprint of Simon & Schuster, Inc.
1230 Avenue of the Americas
New York, NY 10020

For information about special discounts for bulk purchases, please contact Simon & Schuster Special Sales at 1-866-506-1949 or business@simonandschuster.com.

The Simon & Schuster Speakers Bureau can bring authors to your live event. For more information or to book an event contact the Simon & Schuster Speakers Bureau at 1-866-248-3049 or visit our website at www.simonspeakers.com.

ISBN 978-1-5072-0693-5
ISBN 978-1-5072-0561-7 (ebook)

Dedication

To women everywhere.
We are strong. We are bold. We are unstoppable.

Chapter One

"Tuck's been scratched."

Aces Pitcher Pauly Byrne shut her locker with a decisive clang and turned to her coach, eyebrows raised. "What do you mean?"

"There's been a catching change."

That wasn't what she wanted to hear thirty minutes before she took the mound in the last game to clinch the playoffs.

"Is he hurt?"

Coach Slater shook his head grimly, but all he said was, "He's out for tonight." He paused a beat, watching her evenly. "Pratt gets the start."

"*What?* Skip, you know Pratt and I don't—"

"You think I don't know that?" The sweat on the middle-aged man's brow glistened in the fluorescent lights. "With Tuck out and Sheldon hurt, I got no other option."

"But, Skip, c'mon. There are scouts in the stands, and Pratt's unreliable. Just last week, he showed up late, smelling like a brewery, and you said—"

"I know what I said." He held up a hand to stop her. "Doesn't matter. He's all we got. Make it work, or we ain't gonna make the playoffs"—his expression turned wry—"which means I'll be out of a job and you'll be back in Baltimore shucking crabs by this time next week."

She'd never shucked a crab in her life, and she wasn't interested in starting now. If the only thing standing between Pauly and a shot at an Independence League championship was throwing six innings to douchebro Ian Pratt, she could handle that. The question was, could he?

Pauly left the private dressing room the equipment manager had converted from an oversized broom closet three seasons ago, when she'd joined the Arlington Aces. Being the only woman in the Independence League had its perks. She gathered her thoughts, put on her game face, and headed for the clubhouse down the hall.

She stalked straight over to Pratt, ignoring the snorts of protest from some of the bare-assed rookies still getting changed. They didn't have anything she hadn't seen before.

"Pratt, a word."

Her teammates turned. A few made goofy noises, suggesting Pratt was in trouble.

He glanced at her over the eagle tattoo on his left shoulder, with only a towel slung indecently low on his narrow hips. "Do I need to be dressed for this?"

"Doesn't faze me either way."

He shrugged, took his time pulling on his compression shorts, and finally dropped the towel and moved toward her like a burly, surly-faced snail.

"Let me guess. You talked to Coach."

"Yep." She dropped her fists to her hips. "You up for this?"

"I'm up for anything." He grinned his cocky, self-proclaimed "chick-magnet" grin that only made Pauly clench her jaw. Then he stared her down stone cold. "The question is, are you?"

She narrowed her eyes. This wasn't some kegger at the community college or a bonfire bender on the outskirts of Arlington. This was the last regular-season game. The last chance to clinch a playoff spot. The annual "Dads Day at the Ballpark," which meant her father had made the trip all the way from Baltimore. *And*, there were scouts in the stands. "So help me God, Pratt, if you fuck this up, I'm going to—"

"I'm not going to fuck anything up." His bright blue eyes turned icy. "How 'bout you just worry about putting the goddamn ball over the goddamn plate?"

She sucked in a breath and puffed out her chest. "Like last week, when I struck out seventeen batters and didn't allow a single run? Oh, and I was named the Independence League Pitcher of the Week. Like that?"

Pratt lifted his chin and flared his nostrils.

Idiot.

"Hey, hey, hey, hey, hey." Team Captain and first baseman Sam Sutter's voice broke through, reminding her they had an audience. Twenty-two teammates glared and gaped at them. "Pratt, quit jerking her chain. Byrne, give him a chance."

Pauly exhaled then smiled sweetly, her teeth grinding together so much it nearly hurt. "Just making sure we're on the same page."

Ian snorted, rolled his eyes, and lumbered back to his locker.

At this point, Pauly would settle for them being on the same chapter.

Unfortunately, history wasn't on their side. Pratt's framing technique sucked compared to Mason's, and his pickoff moves were about as accurate as her screwball thrown blindfolded. The one and only time he'd caught for her during a game last season, she'd walked four batters, thanks to borderline calls, and ended up belly down on the mound to avoid being drilled by his failed pickoff attempt.

An hour later, out on the field, she was horrified to find they weren't even reading the same book.

"Did you even look at the scouting report?" she asked from behind her glove, concealing her frustration over a 2-1 score and loaded bases from the eyes of the crowd.

"Fuck the report." Ian stopped short of the mound. "You're shaking off everything I call."

"Because you don't know what you're calling!" Out of the corner of her eye, she saw Coach climbing the dugout steps. She didn't need him coming out here and ripping her a new one. Worse, she didn't need to get pulled from the game in the second inning with scouts in the stands. She could do this. She could recover.

Pauly glanced at Coach and held him off with a nod.

"I know I'm not calling low and inside when the guy's babying his right flank." Pratt leaned in closer, smirking. "Your precious report didn't say anything about an injury. Did it?"

No. But Pratt didn't have a medical degree either. She trusted the scouting report a heck of a lot more than she trusted him. Especially since he'd just attempted to pickoff the runner on third. *Who* does *that?* Yadier Molina, that was who, and Pratt wasn't fit to shine Molina's cleats. She growled into her mitt.

"Relax," he said, all cheesy grin and easy charm now, laying a conciliatory hand on her shoulder. "Don't take it so seriously."

God, he really was an idiot. She shrugged him off, practically snarling. "This is not a game, Pratt!"

His brows rose. "Last time I checked, it was."

"Yeah, well, not for me." Not if she ever wanted to make it out of indie ball and into the minor leagues.

"Let's go." The umpire loomed over Pratt's shoulder. "Time's up."

"I'm sticking with the report," she said.

"Of course, you are." Pratt backpedaled toward home plate, getting in one last shot. "Don't say I didn't warn you."

. . .

After the game, Pauly sat at a high-top table in the middle of Foley's Bar and Grill throwing eye-daggers at the back of Pratt's head. "I can't pitch to that asshole."

Five minutes ago, Pratt had moved from the pool tables to the bar, where he tossed back a beer and flirted with the bartender.

"You just did," her father said.

"Yeah, and my ERA suffered."

"But you won the game, and you're playoff bound."

Ed Byrne popped a cheese-smothered tater tot into his mouth like winning was all that mattered, but Pauly knew better. Her father had invested almost half his life in making her a female baseball phenom, working multiple jobs to support her dream of making it to the MLB. Win or no win, she hated that she'd given up four runs with scouts in the stands.

"Maybe Mason'll be back for playoffs," she said hopefully. "Maybe it was a false positive."

"Do you really believe that?"

"It's possible."

"It's also possible he's fallen off the wagon again and he's not going to be back at all, which means Pratt is your catcher, and you've got to deal."

She growled.

"Don't sweat this, P. You're a good enough pitcher to get the job done no matter what the circumstances are. And think of it this way: You only have to tolerate him for—what? Ten more games max, if you make it to the championship. You'll throw—what? Four games. More like two or three if the rotation is strong. Put your game face on, and ride this season out. If you're lucky, you'll win a championship. If you fall short, you've still got next season."

But after that, she was shit out of luck. At 25, she only had one more year of playing eligibility in the Independence League. One more year to win the championship that had been eluding her for almost four seasons. One more year to turn the head of a minor-league scout.

Reaching across her plate of un-sauced chicken wings, she snatched a tater tot off the edge of her father's plate. "Sometimes it feels like I'm running out of time."

"Because you are," he said thoughtfully. "I know it's not something we like to talk about, but maybe it's time." He leveled her with a sympathetic but serious look. "What happens after baseball, P?"

"I don't know," she said, forcing the tot down her throat and reaching for another. From where she sat, there wasn't life after baseball. At least, not a life she wanted to live. What would that even look like? Teaching history? That's what her degree was in. Just thinking about that felt like giving up on herself and her dreams, ticking clock or not.

"I was poking around the Holymount site the other day." Her father's voice sounded tight, and he paused for a drink of soda before continuing. "There was a job posting for a pitching coach."

Pauly stopped the second tot just short of her mouth as she let her father's words sink in. "You think I should apply?"

"I think you should *think* about it." He stared at her long and hard, stirring up a sense of dread inside her. "P, I believe in you. I've supported you every step of the way. Emotionally. Financially. You name it. But I'm getting old, and I'm tired. Your mother and I are really looking forward to the day when you can stand on your own two feet. You know what I mean?" He frowned. "Please, don't take that the wrong way."

Her exhale was shaky. "I know what you mean." Making $1,000 a month, six months a year, playing indie ball in Pennsylvania and giving pitching lessons back home in Baltimore during the off-season wasn't enough for her to be self-sufficient. The most she'd ever filed for income tax was $8,500 one year. That's why her parents still worked multiple jobs when they should've been slowing down and considering their retirements.

"I still believe you might get a shot at the minors, but we can't ignore the fact that less than 4 percent get their contracts purchased. We can't ignore history, either." He frowned. "Four seasons ago, we never imagined you'd still be in Arlington, but here we are."

"Because I haven't won a championship yet. If I win, they aren't going to be able to brush me off as a novelty."

"So win." He flashed his pearly whites. "But just in case the minor leagues still don't come a-knocking, give a thought to what happens *after* baseball." He smiled and nudged her elbow. "Being the first woman baseball coach in NCAA history wouldn't be too shabby, either."

No. But if her alma mater was looking for a pitching coach now, didn't it stand to reason they would want the coach to start next season? The idea of hanging up her cleats at all, let alone a season early, made her feel sick.

Pauly set the tater tot on her plate and looked at her hands, folded in her lap. They were clammy and sore. Probably from clenching her mitt and strangling the ball during today's outing. If she kept on giving up four runs a game, no minor-league team was going to be interested anyway.

She exhaled and forced herself to consider everything her father had been saying. "Even if I was interested in the Holymount position, I've only ever coached kids."

"Playing experience counts. You'd be coming in hot off the field, which would make you more relevant than a lot of applicants. And if you end this season with a championship, that'll round out your resume."

She shifted her line of sight and glared at the back of Pratt's head again. His blond hair pointed and curled every which way but flat. And his laugh. Too loud. Too long. Put on. She wanted to smack him upside the head and tell him to get some control.

"Not *if*, Dad. *When*. I want that championship so bad I can taste it." She didn't take her eyes off Pratt. "I just don't want to pitch to that asshole."

"But you will. You'll find a way. Because you're Pauly Byrne, and that's what you do." Pride infiltrated his grin. "You found a way to become the first woman pitcher to win a high school baseball championship, the first to play NCAA baseball, the first to win an NCAA baseball championship, and you're the *only* woman currently playing in the Independence League. You did it all despite your gender and the color of your skin. Need I say more?"

She smiled, secure in the confidence her father had in her. "Nope. I got the message loud and clear."

"Good. Now, go talk to your catcher and fix whatever's broken between you."

"I'd rather kill him."

"Wouldn't you rather win a championship?"

"I can do both."

Her father chuckled. "You'll enjoy the championship much more if you're not celebrating in jail."

"Good point."

She looked at Pratt again. She wasn't going to let anyone stand in her way of winning a championship, especially when she believed winning was the one thing she could do to get a minor-league team to take a chance on her. If she had to throw to Pratt to win, so be it. Somehow, she would make it work.

And if it didn't work, she knew the perfect little mound of dirt where she could hide his body.

• • •

Ian Pratt smiled at the pilsner glass sliding toward him. The quality Belgian wheat ale reminded him of liquid sunshine, and there was nothing he liked better than a cold beer on a hot day, except maybe drinking the cold beer at Foley's after winning his first ball game as a starting catcher.

"Praaatt!" Sanchez rolled by the bar with his hand raised.

Ian slapped the hell out of it. "'Sup, Sexy?" It was a point of pride that Ian had bestowed nicknames on every member of his team. Sexy Sanchez. Super Sutter. Crazy Carlyle.

"We pulled that one out of our asses," Sanchez said. "You and Byrne had me worried there for a minute."

Ian's grin faltered. He'd given a nickname to everyone except her. After three and a half seasons of her ball-busting, holier-than-thou, my-way-or-the-highway attitude, he'd made it a habit not to talk to or about Pauly Byrne. Until today, when he didn't have a choice.

Sanchez grabbed a fresh beer off the bar, flashing his pearly whites at the bartender, Mandy, and then he folded into the crowd, probably heading back to the pool tables. Ian would be following real soon.

"To my first start with the Aces," Ian said, returning his attention to his father, who was sitting beside him, belly up to the bar. Ian lifted his pilsner glass and tapped it against his dad's tumbler of whiskey. "Glad you crawled outta that dark house and into the light to see it."

Ray Pratt grunted and raised his drink to his mouth. He'd looked older lately. Sickly, even, although there was nothing technically wrong with him. He rarely laughed anymore. Not that he'd ever been a jolly man, but a few drinks used to at least relax the lines around his lips and eyes. Getting old sucked. And Ian was going to fight that serious shit every step of the way.

"Hey, Ugly! Pace yourself."

Ian wasn't the only Ace to hand out nicknames. He grinned at Giovanni Caceres, who rolled through the bar with the team owner's sister, Helen Anne Reed, on his arm.

"Don't you worry about my pace," Ian said. "Unless you're trying to keep up with me."

Helen Anne shook her head wildly as they passed. "He'll be passing on that little trip to your hunting camp, too," she said sweetly.

Caceres looked meek and in love, and Ian felt sorry for the sap. "I didn't want him there anyway," he said, only half teasing.

Choosing a woman over his hunting camp? That wouldn't happen to Ian until hell froze over. No matter how pretty she may be.

Speaking of women … Down the bar, next to his dad, a fun-looking pair tried to get Mandy's attention. The redhead noticed Ian, and she smiled. He smiled back to be polite. Then, he caught Mandy's attention and bought the ladies their first round.

"You're having a good day," his dad said, sounding as flat as usual.

"I'm having a *great* day." How else would you describe clinching a divisional playoff spot *and* having three days off before you had to be on the field again? "You know what would make this day even better? If you'd come up to camp with me and the guys for a little fun."

Ray grunted. "Ain't got time for that."

"Whaddya mean you ain't got time? You're self-employed. Put the closed sign in the garage window and come fishin' with your son for a few days."

"If I don't work, I don't get paid."

That hadn't seemed to bother the guy—who'd been a mechanic only when he'd felt like it—for the last twenty years.

"Seriously?" When his father didn't volunteer more, Ian added, "Suit yourself. That's where I'll be." With a few cases of Corona and enough pork rinds to cover three squares a day.

Ray winced on a mouthful of whiskey. Ian couldn't remember his dad ever having trouble swallowing hard liquor. If Ian had ever been the kind of guy who liked to get into serious conversations with people, he would've asked if everything was okay. Instead, he straightened on his stool and smiled at Mandy. "What are you doing this weekend?"

She rolled her eyes. "Moving out of Dan's place and finding somewhere else to crash before Bella's dad drops her off."

Ian frowned. He knew Dan from high school, and the guy had had a temper even way back then. Getting out was good for

Mandy, but Ian didn't like the idea of her scrambling for a place to stay when her little girl was coming to town. "You know what? Here." He grabbed his key ring from his pocket and wrestled his condo key free. "I'm gonna be gone for three days. Crash at my place. That'll give you some breathing room."

"I couldn't."

"You can. Think about how much fun Bella will have playing *Mario Cart* on a sixty-inch screen." He smiled and nudged the key closer. "Plus, I got a freezer full of Klondikes."

She exhaled, closed her hand around the key, and said, "Thank you, Ian. Three days. I'll pay you rent or something."

"No need. Save your money for the new place."

She smiled, pocketed the key, and patted his hand before moving down the bar to wait on someone else.

Beside him, Ian's dad sniffed. "Better think twice before gettin' involved with somebody who's got a kid."

"She's just a friend."

"That's what you say about all of 'em."

Ian chuckled. "This time I mean it."

"Is this seat taken?"

Ian set his glass down and looked at the open barstool beside him. Joe Morley, a local guy about his dad's age, stood waiting for an invitation.

"Waiting there for you," Ray said.

Joe nodded and slid onto the stool, bumping Ian with his elbow in the process. "How you guys doin'?"

"Never better," Ian said. "Aces are headed to the postseason."

"Good for you, man. Hopefully I'll make it to a game." Joe ordered a Budweiser from Mandy and then folded his hands atop the bar. "So, Ray, you're just the man I wanted to see. Are you still interested in selling the Thunderbird?"

Ian laughed. Of all the stupid things ... "Whoever told you he's selling the T-bird has a few screws loose."

Ray leaned forward and said, "*I* told him."

Ian looked at his father, who wouldn't look at him.

"If you're selling, I'm buying," Joe said.

"He's not selling," Ian said, trying to maintain his good-natured composure stuck in the middle of this idiotic conversation.

Ray leaned forward again, bypassing Ian. "Let's talk about this another time, Joe."

What the hell? Ian polished off his beer and pushed his glass forward for a third.

"Okay, but don't go selling it to somebody else before you talk to me. I'm serious." Joe slid a business card across the bar in front of Ian. "I'll pay top dollar."

Ray agreed.

For fifteen minutes, Ian seethed and weathered small talk while Joe babied his only Budweiser. When the guy finally got up and left the bar, Ian turned to his dad. "You love that car. Why would you even think about selling it?"

"Your mother loved that car."

"Exactly."

Tooling around town in the T-bird with the top down when his mother had been home on leave was one of Ian's favorite memories. The idea of Joe—or anyone else—behind the wheel of that car, made him sick.

"You're not selling," Ian said again, laughing, because this had to be a joke.

"My name's on the deed. I'll do as I please." Ray wiped a hand across his mouth. "I need the money more than I need the car."

"For what?" Ian suspected blackjack or the racetrack had something to do with it.

Ray shot the rest of his whiskey and set his keys on the bar to pull out his wallet. "I'm behind on some bills."

Ian stared at the gold 1965 Thunderbird key. "Dad, if you need help, you know you can come to me. Right?"

Indie ball paid squat, but landscaping in the off-season kept Ian in the black. He wasn't rich, but he wasn't hard up either. He could manage to slip his dad a hundo a month to help pay off his debts.

Ray shook his head and slid off the stool. "I don't need your help. I need you to quit poking around in my business. You hear me? Go on and have fun. That's what you should be doing." He grabbed his keys off the bar and added, "I'm going home to nap."

Ian didn't usually need a push toward fun, but as he watched his father leave the bar, worry crowded out the party instinct. And that wouldn't do. So he polished off his beer and raised a finger to catch Mandy's attention. Something stronger would right his mood before he headed back to the pool tables. A high-ABV bock maybe? Or a bourbon with a chaser of stout.

Mandy folded her tatted arms on the bar and leaned in. "What can I getcha? On the house." She patted her pocket where his condo key now rested.

Free beer was sweet, but his head just wasn't in the right place. "How much do you think a 1965 Thunderbird is worth?"

She laughed. "Hell if I know. It's definitely more than I have."

"Me too," he said thoughtfully.

"You lookin' to buy a car?"

"Something like that."

"My girlfriend, Tami, works at the credit union. I can get you the loan officer's name if that'll help."

Ian smiled, knowing that wasn't going to help one bit.

"I know something that could help," said a familiar female voice behind him, and Ian shortened his neck like a turtle to guard his jugular.

"Gimme your strongest draught," he said to Mandy, before he turned to face Pauly Byrne.

Her long black hair frizzed out through the hole in her baseball cap, but that was the only thing about her that wasn't under strict control. Flawless, dark skin added to the intensity. Even her gray eyes pierced through him like they could burn him alive.

"So *now* you're interested in helping me?" Because it would've been nice for her to have attempted to work with him during the game, instead of sending him back to the plate using an impressive array of murderous looks, one of which was wrinkling into place right now.

"I'm trying to get past today." Her words were slow and deliberate, like everything else she did. Three and a half seasons on the same team, and he'd gotten to know at least that. That *and* the painfully obvious fact she thought he sucked at catching.

He wondered if she ever thought about their very first bullpen, when he'd tried to break the ice by treating her like any other teammate in need of some constructive criticism.

"Don't slouch after a bad pitch," was all he'd said. Why tip off batters to her frustration, letting them know they'd gotten into her head?

"I just won an NCAA championship," she'd said snottily. "I think I know what I'm doing."

The way she'd looked at him, like he was a waste of a roster spot, some townie without her baseball pedigree ... Fuck that. He'd pulled back immediately, but he'd ended up mentioning the slouch to Coach Slater when Coach had asked for Ian's opinion on the bullpen. Of course, when Coach Slater brought up the slouch a few weeks later, Byrne had acted like it was valuable information she was hearing for the first time.

Yeah. She wasn't the only one trying to get past something.

"Well, I'm trying to enjoy today," he said. "We won. Remember?"

Overhead, the television flickered teasers for the 11:00 news and, as if on cue, a shot of Pauly on the mound with a ticker running across the bottom proclaiming, "Female Phenom Clinches Playoff Slot for Aces."

He swallowed an acerbic comment and swatted her forearm with the back of his hand before he pointed at the TV. "See? You're the only one in this whole damn town focusing on the negative."

She stood stock-still, patiently watching the silent newscast. A closed-mouth look he couldn't decipher registered on her face. Meanwhile, with his foot propped on the barstool rung, his leg bounced like mad.

"I'm not being negative," she said, her tone matter-of-fact. "I'm being critical. Of myself. I thought you of all people could appreciate that." When she looked at him, challenge flashed in her steely eyes.

Oh yeah, she remembered that bullpen as well as he did.

"Listen. Not to change the subject," she said with a barely discernable eye roll. "But I overheard you say you want to buy a car, and I know how you can get some extra cash."

It was a reminder his father was trying to sell the T-bird. For all Ian knew, Ray was discussing the sale with Joe right now.

He glanced over his shoulder at the people crowding the bar but didn't see his father or Joe. Still, that didn't put his mind at ease. "Fine. I'll play along. How can I make some extra cash?" he asked, mostly because he was curious about her endgame.

"If we win a championship, you'll get five grand."

"You're going to pay me five grand if we win?"

"No, but the Reeds will." When he didn't react, she added, "It's in our contracts."

Huh. He'd forgotten about that. He was pretty sure five thousand dollars wasn't enough to buy the Thunderbird—or keep his dad from selling it—but it was a start. "Thanks for the information," he said.

He was itching to get back to his care-free normal, but Pauly didn't leave. She stood there beside him in a baggy sweatshirt and jeans that looked low-key enough, but her expression was stone-cold sober. "Pratt ..." She climbed onto the empty stool beside him. "If we want to win a championship, we're going to have to work on our relationship."

He made a sour face. "I didn't know we had a relationship." In fact, he'd been trying damn hard for the last three and a half seasons to not have anything to do with her at all.

"We don't, and that's the problem." She leaned closer, staring at him so intently, the right side of his face heated. "We don't have to be friends, but we need to respect each other as teammates."

Wasn't that the kicker? If he'd cared one bit about working on their relationship, he would've called her out for being a hypocrite. Instead, he winked at Mandy as she slid him a beer, an extra-dark bock by the looks of it.

Pauly made a disgusted sound in the back of her throat. "I don't know how you drink as much as you do. And during the season! Can he get a water too?"

Ian shook off Mandy, but she'd already turned her back on them. "I don't want a water," he said.

"You'll thank me later."

"I won't."

"See? No respect." She clasped her hands together on the bar and exhaled. "We have three days off, Pratt. That's three days to get our shit together."

He ignored her and drank his beer.

"We need to spend some time together," she said.

God, he couldn't think of anything he wanted to do less. "Ooh. Sorry. I'm leaving town for a few days."

Her face twisted, and the expression was a cross between heartbroken and straight pissed. "Why am I not surprised? Of course, you're leaving town. Better than staying here and trying to work out the kinks."

His kinks. He was the one with the kinks. That was how she saw it. No way in hell was he going to skip three days at camp to stay in Arlington and suffer through seventy-two hours of Pauly Byrne telling him what to do and how to do it.

"Byrne," he said, smiling like he meant it. "Relax. You'll pitch better next time. We don't need to do anything drastic like go around joined at the hip."

"You don't get to tell me to relax, Pratt. Not when you're the problem. I want to win this championship. Don't you?"

An hour ago, he would've been noncommittal, but the bonus money may have changed things. With five grand in his pocket, he could help his dad—whether Ray wanted the help or not. Ian drank again. He held the maple-tinged liquid in his mouth and breathed until he could smell the syrup.

Pauly slapped her palms on the bar and growled. "This is exactly what's wrong with us. We don't communicate. We need to learn to communicate if we want to win."

"You're the one who chased me off the mound." He shook two fingers in front of her face. "*Twice*."

Before she could respond, Sanchez leaned against the bar on the other side of Ian. "The fucking service sucks back there. Mandy," he called, shaking his empty glass. "Can you help a brother out?"

Byrne exhaled.

"Hey," Sanchez said, smiling past Ian to Pauly. "You guys strategizing?"

"Something like that," Ian said, to which Pauly grunted her disgust.

Sanchez must've caught on to her sour mood, because he looked at her a beat longer, and then said, "You know what Ace needs? A little man-camp madness."

Ian sucked in a breath and made a face that said, *Shut your mouth*.

Byrne saw it. "What's man-camp madness?"

Ian shook his head.

Sanchez's lips kept flapping. "Whenever we have a day off, we head up to Pratt's camp and blow off some steam."

"Really?" Pauly looked back and forth between them. "It's a team thing?"

Ian couldn't read the expression on her face. "Sort of. But It's probably not *your* thing. Lots of beer. Lots of fishing."

She kept her stormy eyes trained on him. "And *that's* where you're going this weekend?"

"Yep."

"You should come," Sanchez said, and then he escaped with a smile and his beer.

Ian wanted to clobber him. "You don't have to come."

"Oh, I'm coming," she said sharply. "We have a championship to win."

Great. Camp was his happy place. But after three days straight with Pauly Byrne, he wasn't sure what it would be.

Chapter Two

The next morning, Pauly stopped by the mostly deserted stadium. She wanted to get in a quick workout before she was stuck in the woods for seventy-two hours. She just hoped three days at a hunting camp didn't end up being as painful as it sounded.

No pain, no gain, she reminded herself.

At the end of the long main corridor beneath the stadium, light slipped out of the weight-room window. Pauly opened the door and saw pitcher Louie Flynn in the middle of leg presses.

"You started without me," she said.

"Just getting warmed up," Flynn said through clenched teeth. Then he let out a loud groan followed by a puff of air when the weights hit the deck.

Pauly dropped her duffle and inhaled deeply. "Look how peaceful this is."

Flynn sat and swiped a towel over the back of his neck. He was a long, lean, left-handed closer, which would've made him enough of an anomaly all by itself without adding the "married to another man" part.

"And for once it'll be peaceful when I get home, too," he said.

Pauly glanced at the gold band on his ring finger as she climbed aboard the treadmill. Had a whole year really gone by since she'd been "best man" in Flynn's wedding? "You guys okay?"

Flynn laughed. "Yes. I didn't mean it like that. I meant Craig won't be bitching about me spending too much time in the weight room ogling other guys, because there aren't any here."

"He knows you don't really ogle, though, right?" She gave him a look. "You don't. Right?"

"Do *you*?"

Pauly settled into a gentle jog. Flynn was the closest thing she'd ever had to a best friend, but that didn't mean she answered every one of his questions honestly. "If I do, it's for purely utilitarian purposes. Like figuring out who has the most powerful legs and if that makes him any faster, or who has the most defined arms and if that makes him throw farther."

"Mm-hmm," Flynn said, before he laid back and readied for more presses. "Sure. Utilitarian purposes." He popped a skeptical eyebrow, but his lips tipped up in the start of a grin.

Pauly grinned, too. Only Flynn would recognize the fine line she walked between being a ballplayer and a woman. She didn't want to find any of her teammates attractive, but sometimes she did. Fortunately, the finest ones—physically speaking—tended to be the biggest assholes. Like Pratt.

"There's nothing wrong with noticing someone's hot," she said. "I see good-looking people all the time. That doesn't mean I'm going to jump them."

"Preach." Flynn growled the word, and then, when the weights hit the deck with a shudder and a clang, he added, "But try tellin' that to my husband."

"See, that's why I'm not getting involved with anyone until my playing days are over." Which was coming down the pipe faster than an Aroldis Chapman fastball, unless she got picked up by a minor-league team. And that got her thinking about life after baseball again.

Pauly increased the incline and ran harder.

"Who you kidding?" Flynn hung the towel around his neck and headed across the room to the water station. "You're not getting involved with anybody because you're The Ice Queen. Isn't that why they call you Ice?"

She rolled her eyes. "They call me Ace, smart-ass."

"My bad. Switched up a couple letters." He laughed, but she couldn't. She'd been called Ice Queen before, too. And while that usually didn't bother her, it did make her wonder.

"Do you think I'm an ice queen?" she asked, breathing a little harder, feeling the sweat roll down her back.

"No. I think you're badass."

She grinned.

"What are you doing with your time off … besides this?" Flynn asked.

So she wasn't the only one excluded from Pratt's man-camp madness. "Well—"

"Better not be baseball related."

"It is," she said, not *un*-defensively.

He groaned. "Why don't you let me fix you up? Craig's always bitching about this place being a meat market, but his law firm is just as bad. What are your specs?"

Pauly laughed. She hadn't dated in years. She didn't have specs; she had cobwebs.

"Seriously. Tell me what you like, and Craig and I will set something up for tomorrow night."

Sufficiently warmed up, she killed the machine and hopped off. "Actually, I'm going out of town for a few days."

"Home?"

She shook her head. "To Pratt's cabin." And because that sounded seedy all by itself, she clarified, "With some of the guys."

Flynn frowned. "Like a team thing?"

She hesitated at the disappointment in his eyes. "Sort of. Sanchez invited me. You should come, too."

"And explain to Craig why I'm spending my days off in the woods with the guys he's always worrying about? No, thanks. But … it would've been nice to have been asked."

Pauly nodded. "I know. I was an afterthought, too. Which is a big part of why I'm going. The other part is to get at Pratt."

"Oh, *really?*" Flynn's brows lifted with interest.

"Not like that." *God, no.* "We need to find a way to work better."

"So you're going to bond with him over beers?"

She shrugged. "I guess." But she didn't drink, so that might make things a little harder. "I also have a trunk full of gear and equipment, and I'm bringing my laptop with video and scouting reports. We won't get bored."

Flynn gaped at her, and then he whistled. "They're gonna *love* that."

"They might."

"Sure they will." He chuckled. "Three days off, and you're going to roll up with a trunk full of teaching materials."

"What else am I going to do up there?"

"You could try to relax and have a good time."

"*Camping?*" she asked, her tone so incredulous it made Flynn laugh harder.

"My offer still stands."

A little jolt in the driest part of her made the idea sound tempting, but her baseball-centric brain knew a blind date wouldn't help her win a championship.

"I'm going to prove you wrong, Flynn," she said determinedly. "When I come back, all my hard work is going to pay off. Pratt and I are going to be working like a well-oiled machine."

Flynn cackled. "Good luck with that."

• • •

Ian sat an open beer on the porch railing and ambled down the steps of the log cabin that had been in his family since his grandfather had won the place in a poker match. She was here. And by the look of her furrowed brow, she was plenty pissed about something. Not that that was anything out of the ordinary.

Still, she couldn't be half as pissed as Ian was—Sanchez and the other guys hadn't even shown up yet.

Pauly slammed her car door and glared at the white Nissan. Or formerly white anyway. Mud speckled the doors of the sedan and caked the tires. She wore jeans ripped at the knees with frayed patches of denim high on her thighs, and a red T-shirt that clung in all the right places. A gray hoodie was tied around her waist, but it didn't cover anything. In fact, it just drew his attention to her narrow waist and curvy ass. All he could see was a woman instead of a ballplayer, and that soured his mood even further.

"A little warning would've been nice, Pratt."

"It's just mud. It'll come off. Rel—"

She held up a finger. "Don't tell me to relax. I already got that lecture today."

He grinned, liking the idea that somebody had backed him up even if they hadn't meant to.

"Don't," she said.

"Don't what?"

"Don't go thinking you're right because somebody else told me to relax. I can't."

"No effing kidding," he growled under his breath. "You got bags?"

She ducked into the backseat, giving him a prime shot of the Aces logo pulled tight across her ass. A low hum of awareness spread across his belly. When he got his hands on Sanchez, he was going to strangle him.

"There's more in the trunk," she said, her voice muffled.

Suspicion made him falter. "How much more?"

She emerged from the depths of the backseat with a duffle that could've easily held everything she needed for two nights and three days in the woods. "Just the essentials. Equipment, laptop, food." She ticked them off on her fingers.

"And here I thought the essentials were beer, pork rinds, and live bait." He pointed to the already opened case of Corona on the front porch.

She made a sour face.

Ian followed her around to the trunk and stared at its contents. A milk crate full of Power Plus Protein powder and bars caught his eye. "Haven't you ever been camping before?"

"I'm a black woman from Baltimore. What do you think?"

He laughed. "I think you're in for a rude awakening."

"You too," she said with a confident nod and a couple smacks to what looked like a laptop bag. Then, she gathered up a few more things, leaving the crate for him.

He shook his head, unwilling to think too hard about what his rude awakening might be, and then he grabbed the crate, shut the trunk, and powered back to the porch, passing her and that ass before he did a double take.

"I brought my laptop so we can study reports and get transaction updates," she said. "How often do you check the league website? They upload it daily. Coach Slater tipped me off a couple seasons ago, and I've been checking it ever since. You should too. Why prepare for a batter whose contract has been purchased, you know?" She said it all without a breath and with way too much enthusiasm. "I also have a video library going back three seasons. And if we have any questions, Skip is always available by phone."

So *this* was his rude awakening.

Ian stopped on the bottom step and faced her. Reports? Transactions? Videos? It was all bad enough without imaging phone calls to Coach Slater on their days off.

By the time Pauly realized he'd stopped, they were a few measly inches from a collision.

"Oh!" Her wide, silver eyes met his, defusing his annoyance just a bit.

On the field, when she'd refused to step off the mound to meet him, they'd stood nose to nose, but on the steps, like this, Ian had a good six inches on her. He liked having the edge. "No phones up here."

She blinked. "Really?"

"No reception."

"Then I can use the landline."

"No landline."

She looked disturbed. "What if there's an emergency?"

"I get reception at the top of the hill about a mile down the road."

She looked at their wooded surroundings, and her pretty mouth fell open. "That's insane." Then her hand slid up the strap of her laptop bag and her knuckles whitened. "What about internet?"

Good question. Overanalyzing the shit out of a *game* wasn't going to help anyone win a championship. That's why Coach Slater had given them three days off. No way was Ian going to spend seventy-two hours in study hall.

What were the chances a city girl would recognize the SatNet dish on the roof?

Oh, what the hell? He would take his chances. "No internet."

Her eyes shifted to the case of beer behind him. "I'm not going to spend the next three days sitting around watching you guys drink." As soon as she said it, she seemed to realize they were missing something. "Where is everybody? Sutter? Caceres?"

If Mason hadn't failed the drug test, she'd be looking for him, too. Because those guys had been in the majors. Those guys were worth her time and respect.

Ian shrugged. "I don't know. Nobody else is here."

"Like nobody else is here *yet*, or nobody is coming at all?"

"Not coming at all," he said, just to mess with her. And then he smiled, because he knew that would really get under her skin.

"I'm outta here." Her eyes flashed, and her nostrils flared. "This was a terrible idea."

"Hey! That's something we can actually agree on."

She yanked the crate from his hands and backed up. "Good luck getting that five grand."

"Good luck getting that car clean." He grabbed his beer off the railing and kept on smiling.

"I really think I hate you." She jammed the crate into the backseat and threw in her bags. "I mean, what did I ever do to you?"

He shrugged, surprised anyone could still be so damn attractive while being so damn annoying. "You tell me."

Their eyes connected in a lethal staring match, and for a second, he expected her to come clean, bring up the bullpen incident, hell, tell him point-blank she thought he sucked. But no, it was all about her. Always had been.

"You're a dick because I'm a woman playing on *your* ball team. Well, get over it, Pratt. It's *my* team. I was the starter long before you." She ripped open the driver's-side door and darted inside.

Her tires spun as she backed out, narrowly missing a tree.

Good riddance.

He polished off his beer and flattened the can beneath his foot. Birds chirped overhead. The wind rustled through the trees. But he couldn't relax.

He whipped out his phone, checked for the satellite connection, and group-texted the guys who should've been there by now.

Pratt: Where u at?

Sanchez: Pittsburgh.

Pratt: WTF?

Carlyle: Met a chick with some friends and a boat ... and Kenny Chesney tickets.

Sanchez: Sorry, man.

Rodrigues: Offer too good to pass up.

Ian fired back with the middle finger emoji and left the group chat. Then, he set his phone on the railing and reached for another beer. Nobody was coming. Half the team had gone home to see family. The other half was spending time with family in Arlington. Which meant he was looking at three days alone. With his thoughts.

Silence roared in his ears, and something akin to fear bubbled up in his chest. He washed it down with a hearty swig.

An image of Byrne, eyes blazing, popped into his head. *Good luck getting that five grand.*

He wasn't going to spend the next three days bored out of his mind, worrying about the Thunderbird and his dad. Nope. Something would work out. Things always worked out. Except when they didn't. He thought about his mom, and the fear welled up again.

On that note, Ian wandered out to the "elbow tree" behind the cabin and sat on the low, horizontal limb that gave the tree its name. Then he stared at the marble plaque that marked the spot where his mother's ashes were buried.

"Am I a dick?" He took another drink and swallowed, weeding through faded memories of his no-bullshit mom. "Of course, I am."

But this time, he had good reason.

"She thinks she's better than me," he said with the bottle paused at his lips.

And when the wind blew, he could've sworn he heard his mother ask, "Is she?"

"At pitching, definitely. But I can hit the shit around her. And I'm a better catcher than she gives me credit for. In fact,"—he lowered the bottle to his knee and rubbed a hand across his mouth—"if she'd just listen once in a while I could help her be even better."

If he wasn't such a dick, he would've texted Pauly exactly that, and then he would've apologized for chasing her away and risking the championship. Instead, he pressed two fingers to his lips and bent to swipe the same two fingers over his mother's name. Then, he headed to the river, where he could cast a line or two before he drove home to Arlington.

Chapter Three

What had she been thinking? No phone. No internet. But, hey, there was plenty of beer and one giant jerk who pushed every button she had.

She should've stayed in town and taken Flynn up on his offer.

Pauly turned the steering wheel, swerving to miss another pothole in the dirt road. Then she leaned out the window and yelled, "God's country, my ass!"

Her phone sprang to life as she crested the hill, blinking and dinging, ringing and beeping. It looked possessed. Apparently, she was out of the dead zone.

She pulled over to inspect the six text messages, three missed calls, one voicemail, and a dozen or so social media notifications, but she didn't get too far before her phone rang again.

"Hey, Dad."

"Did you see it?"

"See what?"

"Holymount gave you a shout out on Twitter."

"Why?"

"For making it to the divisional playoffs. You didn't see it?"

"No. I've been out of phone range."

"Where the hell are you?"

"I'm …" She stared out her windshield at miles of nothing broken up by thick patches of trees. *In hell.* A picture of Pratt with a pitchfork popped into her head. Only, he wasn't red, and he was jacked with muscles she didn't want to be ogling. *Yep. Hell.* "I made a wrong turn, but I'm back on track now."

"Good. Make sure you retweet that. I already did, and I told your brothers to do it, too. The publicity helps." With her brand—something her dad had been encouraging her to cultivate for years. But publicity didn't win championships.

"Okay." She exhaled and looked in the rearview mirror. After the debacle back at Ian's camp, her championship hopes were dwindling. Maybe she was nuts not to consider that coaching position.

"How's the arm feel?"

"Good." But that was the least of her worries.

Pratt was probably another beer in and glad to be rid of her. The crazy thing was, if he wanted to get rid of her quickly and permanently, helping her look good on the field was the best way to do it. Next chance she got, she would take that approach with him.

"Stay focused," her father said.

"I will."

"Don't let anybody get in your way."

Not even Pratt. *Crap.* She should've stayed at that stupid cabin. She should've stood her ground and proved Flynn wrong like she'd promised. She had enough information saved on her computer to at least make a go of it. And now she had mobile access, which meant she had internet. She could turn on a mobile hotspot, download whatever else she needed, and take it back to camp. Pratt could be a dick all he wanted, but she was going to get through to him.

"Thanks, Dad."

When the call ended, she grabbed her laptop and balanced it between her stomach and the wheel, calling up the league website and heading straight for the latest injury and transaction reports.

Her phone vibrated, and she glanced at the screen to see a text from Flynn:

How's it going?

No way was she going to fess up to this little snag.

Pauly: Great!
Flynn: Liar. What do you think of this?

Below the message was a photo of a man in a suit.

She tapped the pic and made it bigger. The angle was mostly profile, but she could tell he was nice looking. Tall in comparison to his surroundings. Dark. And clean-shaven.

She texted back.

Pauly: Not bad.
Flynn: What's missing?
Pauly: Idk. Doesn't look like the kind of guy who would appreciate a woman who plays baseball.
Flynn: What makes you say that?
Pauly: Just a hunch.
Flynn: Just an excuse.
Pauly: Maybe.
Flynn: Back to the drawing board. (BTW, Craig says you're picky.)

Picky? Maybe. Scared? Probably. But it wasn't like experience hadn't given her reason to be.

Pauly set her phone aside and refocused on her laptop, scanning the transaction report, feeling a jolt of jealousy at every contract sold to an MLB team. These guys were part of the lucky 4 percent of Independence League players who moved up. Tough odds, but the odds didn't matter. Her first few seasons, she'd wanted to move up more than she'd ever wanted anything. And she'd believed a minor-league offer was at the end of every win she'd pitched. Unfortunately, with each passing year and no interest, wanting it became more and more demoralizing, and believing it became harder. Still, she dreamed it could happen, even though it probably wasn't realistic now.

Especially not with Pratt behind the plate.

Wait a minute. She scrolled back to a name she nearly missed. *Teddy Willman. Right flank injury. Fourteen-day disabled list.*

Her memory replayed scenes from yesterday. Pratt insisting on low and away. Pratt rushing the mound to explain. And Pauly going against his advice. *I'm sticking with the report.* Willman's RBI hadn't seemed like much at the time, but it had started something, something that had led to her giving up four freaking runs. And, yeah, they'd won the game, but still … Would she have given up fewer runs if she'd given Pratt the benefit of the doubt?

Crap. She reread the notice. *Teddy Willman. Right flank injury.* Just like Pratt had said. But it had been a lucky guess. Right? He couldn't have known for sure.

And then it hit her, like it had in the driveway of the cabin—a memory from her first season with the Aces, her first bullpen, to be exact. Guys milling around to watch a woman throw heat, ready to pass judgment. Her throat constricted at the memory. She'd wanted to impress them, especially the guys who'd spent time in the minor and major leagues. Those guys would be her mentors. Those guys could help her get where they had been. Instead, she got stuck throwing to some townie whose only baseball credits were four years of club ball in college and summers playing in an Arlington rec league. And still, he'd had the audacity to say, "Don't slump your shoulders after a bad pitch." He'd said it loud enough for everyone to hear, too. Pointed out her lack of emotional control. Highlighted her poor performance. And she'd hated him for making her look foolish.

Pauly dropped her forehead to the steering wheel and inhaled. She still hated him, and it had to stop if they were going to win another game, let alone a championship. If she hadn't made up her mind to go back to the camp before, she was making it up now.

Pratt was still a dick, but she'd been one too.

•••

Ian didn't turn around when he heard someone on the dock behind him. He didn't have to. If it had been anybody but Pauly, they wouldn't have driven up the driveway at warp speed, and they most definitely would've asked for a beer by now.

He was oddly relieved she'd come back.

"Teddy Willman is on the DL now with a right flank injury," she said.

Ian smiled, partially vindicated, but he couldn't think of what had happened on the mound without thinking about what had happened in the bullpen. There was a pattern here, a pattern of her not being willing to listen to him. And while she'd acknowledged he'd been right in his assessment of Willman, it wasn't exactly an apology, either.

He kept his focus on the bobber floating atop the silky gray water. "You came all the way back to tell me that?"

"No. I came back to win a championship … but since I'm here, I want to know how you knew about Willman, or if it was just a lucky guess."

He'd put his money on her suspecting the latter. "I saw him twist and flinch as he approached the plate. My bell went off."

"You have a bell?"

"When I'm sober." He raised his beer can. "And I'm always sober on the field."

"I don't have a bell," she said, sounding thoughtful.

"You also don't have a catcher's view. That's why I call things the way I do."

When she didn't say anything, he glanced over his shoulder and found her staring off into the trees.

"I can help you be a better pitcher," he said, facing the water again. "I know that's hard to believe since I'm not some hotshot major leaguer like Mason was, but I got good instincts."

She snorted. "I can't really argue with that. After Willman."

"But you wanna argue with it, don't you?"

"Yeah, I wanna argue it. How am I supposed to put my faith in somebody who shows up late to practices, parties the night before games, and tries to make me look bad every chance he gets?"

"What?" He shifted his weight and angled his body so he could keep the line in position while he faced her and called her on her bullshit. "When did I ever try to make you look bad?"

Hands on hips, posture rigid, she shot him an icy glare. "You've said things, Pratt. Things I've overheard. Things other guys have overheard. Like my fastball can't get the job done. Ring a bell? And you called me out in front of everybody in the bullpen. Remember that?"

"Jesus." He shook his head, rattling his thoughts. "Byrne, Flynn's curveball is crap. I say that all the time, too. Doesn't mean I'm setting him up for failure every time he throws to me. And that bullpen? I was trying to help you. Like I'd help any other pitcher. I'm sorry if you thought I was messing with you." He shook his head again. "You know what I think? That's only half the story. Admit it. You think you're better than me. That's what makes it so hard for you to listen."

Her nose wrinkled, and her nostrils flared. She struggled with her thoughts for the longest time, finally giving up, her arms in the air. "Fine. I think I'm better than you. I've worked my ass off to get here. You don't even know what that feels like. Sutter said you tried out for the team on a whim. A whim! The rest of us were desperate to make this team, and you were just tossing the dice. Must be nice."

It was nice, but he wasn't about to piss her off by saying that. "You got me," he said. "Baseball's just a hobby. Doesn't mean I don't go out there hoping to win every game."

"Hoping and wanting are two different things. I *want* to win a championship."

"So do I."

"For the money?"

"Does it matter?"

She stared at him for a few loaded seconds and then shook her head. "As long as you want it, the reason doesn't matter. At least it doesn't matter to me."

He nodded once and then went back to studying the ripples in the water.

A minute passed. Maybe more. They'd each said their piece and arrived at a small place of commonality. Now, he wondered if she would leave.

"Maybe we could try this again?"

Try what? he almost asked, but he caught her drift. "Sure. Grab a rod."

"Oh, uh …" Pauly shuffled around behind him. "No, thanks. I'll watch." She sat beside him, leaving plenty of space between them, her long legs dangling off the dock, her smooth skin peeking out from between the threadbare jeans. Of all things to find sexy …

He snapped his attention back to the water. They should talk. About what, he wasn't sure. Baseball was the easy answer, but baseball seemed to be a sore spot for them. If they wanted to preserve the truce, maybe they should work up to that. Keep things neutral.

"If you've never been camping, I'm guessing you've never been fishing, either," he said.

"Nope. Doesn't look like I'm missing out on a lot, though. How long does it take to catch something?"

"Sometimes fifteen minutes. Sometimes three hours."

"Three hours?" She laughed. It was a light sound that seemed to bounce off the water and linger in the air, and it was in total contrast to her usually serious demeanor. "You could drive to the grocery store and back in that much time."

He glanced at her and smiled. "Where's the fun in that?"

"I guess, but it doesn't seem very efficient."

"Listen," he said, reaching for his beer. "When you're up here, efficiency is a four-letter word. When you're back on the mound, you can worry about efficiency. Deal?"

She took a big breath and exhaled. "Deal." Then she planted her palms on the dock and leaned back as if she was really going to give this relaxation thing a try.

She still looked stiff as hell though, and he held in a laugh.

They sat like that in silence for a few minutes, his eyes on the bobber and Pauly's face to the sun. Quiet. Peaceful. She wasn't so bad … when he wasn't so bad.

Eventually, the quiet and his curiosity got the better of him. "If you didn't fish and you didn't camp, what'd you do for fun with your family growing up?"

"Baseball tournaments. I started playing travel ball when I was eight. My brothers played, too, so we never took a trip that wasn't baseball related."

"Never?"

She shook her head.

"Damn. That's a lot of baseball."

"Good thing I love it." Her swinging legs cast a wobbly shadow on the water.

"I'm surprised you still do."

"Some days it feels like a job instead of a passion, but I can't imagine doing anything else." She got quiet—so quiet he looked at her.

Frown lines bunched her forehead as she chewed the skin around her thumbnail. She looked concerned. Tormented. Out of the blue, she reminded him of his mother, the way she used to sit at the kitchen table, staring off into space, worrying about heavy things like bills and his failing grades and whatever she'd seen on the evening news. He banished that thought with another mouthful of beer.

"I downloaded the reports when I had internet access up the road," Pauly said.

Ian shook his head. "I'm not surprised."

"Prep is an important part of what we do."

"Prep is an important part of what *you* do. I'd rather wing it."

"You can't wing a championship."

"I wing everything." He set his beer on the dock when the bobber dipped a fraction of an inch.

"Pratt, we have to—"

He shushed her. The bobber dunked, and he whipped the rod and reel into action.

Pauly drew her legs away from the water with a strangled squeal.

The fish broke the surface only to disappear again.

"What should I do?" Pauly asked, jumping to her feet and scrambling out of view. "Do you need me to do anything? Is there a net? I can hold the net."

He laughed. "Just calm the fuck down." In one fluid motion, he stood and pulled the walleye from the water. He glanced behind him and smiled. "You're such a city girl." He held the fish, still on the hook, out to her. "Do you want to touch it?"

"Fool," she said, jumping back, but she laughed, and that made him laugh again.

A half hour ago, he'd been ready to drive back to Arlington and spend three days shooting pool and drinking beer at Foley's. Now, he had another option. He could stay here with her. His bell went off—loudly—but he ignored it.

"You know what I'm going to do?" He put the fish in the cooler and opened another beer. "I'm going to be a gentleman and teach you how to fish."

Her eyes widened, and her expression said, *Like hell you are.*

"What's a matter, Byrne? Worried you won't be any good at it?"

"I'm good at everything I do," she said with attitude to spare, but her sparkling eyes darted back and forth between the rod on the dock and the cooler, like she was questioning herself. "Besides, it doesn't look like it takes much skill."

"Care to put your money where your mouth is?" He grabbed the rod and thrust it at her.

"What's the bet?"

"If you catch a fish in the next hour, I'll read over the reports you downloaded."

"What if my fish is bigger than yours?"

He grinned. "Size doesn't matter."

A saucy smirk brightened her face. "We both know that's not true."

Damn. He nipped his thoughts in the bud before they nosedived. "Take the pole, Byrne, before you lose your nerve."

She took the pole and walked to the end of the dock, where she looked out over the water and then back at him. "There's nothing in here big enough to pull me in, is there?"

"Not as long as you keep your center."

"How do I do that?" She sent a worried look over her shoulder. "You have to actually teach me how to do this, or the bet is off."

"Okay." He took a few steps closer, rubbing his palms on his jeans. Touching her would be the easiest way to show her how to cast the line, but he hesitated. He didn't want to go down that road even a little bit. "See that button on the reel? Press it, keep it pressed, and sidearm the rod to throw the line."

"Okay." Her shoulders rose and fell. Her long hair swayed in the breeze, dropping to the middle of her back, about six inches from her narrow waist. He should've stopped the assessment there, but he lowered his gaze to the curves of her ass, outlined in soft denim. She must've left the sweatshirt in the car.

"Here we go!" With a shout and a jerk, she pulled him out of his trance.

The line sprung free, and the bobber dropped in the river.

"Was that good?" she asked, bouncing on the toes of her running shoes.

He snuck another peek at her ass. "Perfect."

"See?" She tossed him a haughty look. "This is easy."

"Because that's the easy part. Wait until you get something on the line."

She shrugged him off and lowered her ass to the dock.

Thank God.

Ian grabbed a beer from the soft-sided cooler, figuring half-baked and sleepy was better than buzzed and horny any day. Then he took a seat beside her.

A few minutes in, she yawned. "This is boring."

"It's relaxing. Beer?" He offered his.

She made a face. "No."

"Is it the beer or my germs?"

"Both," she said. "I don't know where those lips have been, and alcohol is a dehydrator. I'll take a bottled water."

"Fresh outta spring water, unless you count what's in front of you."

She leaned forward for a closer look with the pole wedged between her legs and both hands wrapped around the shaft. Maybe it was the view coupled with her mention of where his lips had been, but his dirty mind stirred, and his muscles tightened. He pinched the bridge of his nose and inhaled.

"I wouldn't drink that water if you paid me to," she said. "How's the tap?"

"It's well water."

"Gag."

"Have you ever had it?"

"Of course not."

"Then you're in for a treat. We don't soften it, so it's like drinking liquid metal."

"Yum." Her face distorted. "And this is a vacation to you?"

"This is heaven to me." He laid back on the dock and watched the sun disappear behind a cloud.

Time went by. He dozed off, drifting in and out of consciousness. The wind blowing warm across his skin. The occasional bug buzzing softly in his ear. He saw his mother's smile, felt her strong hands on his wrists. "You got a fish," she whispered. "Reel it in." She looked happy. She was happy. He wanted to freeze everything right here so she wouldn't get sad.

"Pratt!" The blood-curdling scream rocketed him into a sitting position, a sense of dread swirling inside him.

Pauly came into focus, kneeling on the dock with her hands strangling the rod. "You sleep like you're dead, dude. I got something! What do I do? How do I keep my center?" Her shrieks mixed with laughter, and the energy of the moment brought him back to earth.

"Give it some line," he said.

"Why would I give it line if I'm trying to bring it in?"

"Because you don't want the line to snap. Give it a little, and then start reeling it in nice and slow. Real smooth."

She was so rigid he worried one yank from the fish and she'd tumble off the dock. But, miracle of miracles, she actually listened to him.

"Okay. I'm reeling." The fish jumped, and she bobbled the rod.

Ian scrambled toward her on his knees, hell-bent on keeping the rod from hitting the water. He reached around her with one hand and caught the grip in midair. With his other hand, he grabbed her waist for balance, pulling her hard against his chest so neither one of them fell.

"Got it," he said. A few strands of her hair kicked up in the wind and grazed his face. Her soft, fresh scent assaulted him. "Got it," he said again, hoping to justify his handsy behavior.

"Yep." She didn't move except to ride the wave of his next breath. And the next.

Everywhere their bodies touched, his nerve endings sparked.

"What about the fish?" she asked, turning her head until his lips were a millimeter from her ear.

"It got away," he said gruffly.

"Crap."

There was no reason to be holding her like this now, soaking up her heat, encouraging the dead-end feelings stirring deep in his belly. So Ian leaned back and put both hands on the rod, while Pauly continued to stare at the water like she wasn't feeling anything but disappointment over losing the fish.

"Do I get another chance?" she asked.

He had to hand it to her ... she didn't rattle easily.

Chapter Four

Pauly locked her eyes on the bobber. Somewhere behind her a beer can cracked open. By her count, that was three beers since she'd set foot on the dock.

"I'm being generous, giving you another chance, so you gotta reel this one in by yourself," Pratt said.

"Fine by me." She didn't want him touching her like that ever again. In fact, she didn't even want to think about it.

Think about baseball. She had enough data stored in her head to keep her busy for hours.

"Custer has been crushing the first or second pitch consistently," she said, mostly to herself.

"Who's Custer?"

"Brett Custer, Charleston's first baseman. You know, the team we're facing in the divisional playoffs?" Ian didn't respond, so she continued. "If Custer gets behind in the count, he almost always strikes out." She adjusted her grip on the rod and rocked her butt back and forth against the hard wood, settling into a more comfortable position. "He also favors fastballs, so I definitely won't be throwing any." She reinforced that with a nod and watched a leaf float atop the rippling water beneath her feet. The air up here smelled clean and sweet, and it was a little bit distracting. "He struggled with the curve earlier this season, so I think that's my best bet. Unless I pitch fast and outside and capitalize on the idea that he's waiting to crush a fastball. If I get him to swing and miss the first pitch, that'll rattle him good. It's risky, though. Don't you think?"

No response.

She glanced behind her. Pratt was sprawled out on the dock with his eyes closed, the beer balanced on his table-top abs. Sun blanketed him from the choppy tips of his blondish hair to the dark soles of his Nike Air Max sneakers. He looked … peaceful. She focused on the undulating swell of his broad chest. Up and down. Up and down. He wasn't breathing deeply enough to be sleeping, which meant he was ignoring her.

Folding a leg beneath her, she refocused on the water. *Whatever.* If she kept talking, the info might penetrate his thick skull.

She cleared her throat. "He also adjusts the Velcro on his batting gloves twice each glove between every pitch, and he spits every third pitch."

"You've gotta be shittin' me," Pratt said. He drawled the words like he was lazy *and* appalled. "Who cares how many times the guy spits?"

"I care. I like to know everything about every batter I face, so I can plan for anything. I don't like surprises."

"You're taking the fun out of it. It's a game, remember?"

"Not for me." It hadn't been "just a game" for a long time. She narrowed her gaze on the bobber. Had it dipped? She tugged on the line but felt no resistance.

"That's your problem, Byrne," Pratt said.

"*You're* my problem."

Ha. He didn't have a comeback this time.

After that, silence stretched out between them, punctuated only by birds singing and bugs buzzing. She switched legs and leaned back on one hand. Every once in a while the water bubbled and sloshed against the bank, making her think something was on her line, but nothing was ever there.

Minutes passed. Maybe hours. She didn't know. She'd left her useless phone in the car. And the longer she sat there, staring at the water, the more time slipped away, folding in on itself until it evaporated. The sun warmed the top of her head and crept down her back, littering her skin with tiny beads of sweat. The light would disappear altogether eventually, but until then, there was absolutely no way for her to measure her progress ... unless she counted heartbeats or breaths. It was an odd state. Unproductive but peaceful.

Eventually, Pauly glanced behind her again. The beer was on the dock now, and Pratt's chest rose and fell in strong, smooth waves. He was out. If Sleeping Beauty had been a man, that's what he would've looked like. Her brain shorted on all the silence and skipped ahead to a magical kiss. Her gaze anchored on his lips, and her body—

No. No. No. No. No. No. No.

She snapped around to face the water. This was nuts. She was all for starting over, trying again, and anything else that would give them an on-field advantage, but right now, they were wasting time. Fishing and napping and daydreaming about stupidly inappropriate kisses weren't going to help them win a championship.

"Hey." She banged on the dock to make sure he heard her. She didn't want to look back again, but when he didn't answer her, she stole a glance.

Pratt stirred, shielding his eyes from the sun and squinting at her. "Got one?"

"No." She faced the water again, because he looked sexily disheveled, lounging there in the sun. "And it's starting to piss me off."

His laugh was low and scratchy as he shuffled around behind her. "Did you check the line to see if you still have bait?"

"No. You didn't tell me to do that."

She reeled in the line and found an empty hook.

He was beside her now, leaning out to grab the line, brushing her elbow with his arm. He'd baked long enough in the midday sun that his cologne radiated off him in warm, delicious waves.

The dock felt too small now, and Pauly tried like hell not to let it bother her. But she hadn't been alone with a guy she wasn't related to—or who wasn't gay—in a good long time.

"Somebody got a free meal," Pratt said.

"Bastards." She stared at the spot where the bobber had been. "I never even felt anything."

"That comes with experience." He ducked behind her to pull a fat worm from the cooler, offering it to her with a smile. "Wanna do the honors?"

Hell no. But she never backed down from a man with a challenge, so she nodded. "Okay."

One brow raised, and his lips quirked. "You sure? You don't look sure."

"Give it, Pratt." She lifted her chin and accepted the worm in her palm with way too much confidence.

Now what? Was she supposed to tie the worm in a knot around the hook or impale it? Decisions, decisions. She opted for the first.

She opted wrong.

"Here. Like this," Ian said, moving closer until he blocked the sun.

Funny, she didn't feel any cooler. His warm breath tickled her temple, and she stared mindlessly at his fingers as they brushed against hers.

"The trick is to spear 'em near the top and then slide 'em up the hook." He guided her hands in tandem with his directions, but he didn't actually hook the worm. "See? Now, give it a go." His voice was soft. His tone was gentle. And every cell in her body urged her to move closer, while her brain screamed for her to run.

Dude. She was the genius who'd said they needed to work on their relationship, but this was crazy.

Pauly gulped and tried to concentrate. She could've sworn her hands were shaking, but when she looked at them, they were perfectly still. Unfortunately, she couldn't say the same for the worm, so she took a breath and hooked it before she lost her nerve.

"Good," Pratt said. "Excellent." His deep voice dripped with encouragement and sex appeal.

She felt lightheaded. Maybe it was the heat. *Please, be the heat.*

"Now, spear it again," he said. "Somewhere in the middle. Leave a little bit dangling to attract the fish. Gotta make it look sexy." He chuckled.

She fumbled with the hook and worm but managed to complete the task. No thanks to him, standing over her, rattling her nerves.

"Perfect," he said. "Now, cast it."

She looked up, and he was smiling, but not the smarmy smile that set her teeth on edge. A wide, genuine smile that crinkled the skin around his eyes and said there was no place he'd rather be than here, teaching a city girl to sacrifice worms to the river gods. She smiled back, feeling like she'd accomplished something meaningful, when they'd barely begun to talk about baseball.

It *had* to be the heat and humidity.

Pratt stepped back, giving her room to cast. She flubbed the first toss but got the bobber into the darker water on the second try. Then she sat and admired her work. It really wasn't hard once you got the hang of it. "Did someone teach you to fish, or did you learn on your own?"

He opened another beer and sat beside her.

Number four.

"My mom taught me." He sounded sad almost, but then he paused for a drink and swallowed on a laugh. "We used to call her the fish whisperer. Damn things literally came to the surface when they heard her voice. She was amazing."

Past tense. "Is she … Did she … pass?"

"A long time ago. Her ashes are buried a couple hundred yards from the house. She loved this place."

Wow. Pauly didn't know what to say. Her eyes roved his face while he stared at the water. Grief lined his cheek and set his jaw. "I'm sorry about your mom," she said. "I think it's really cool she's resting here, and I can see why you love it, too."

He set his beer on the wood beside him and nodded, glancing back and forth between the river and her. "Byrne?" he whispered, and her heart leapt.

"Yeah?"

"You got a fish."

And this time, she reeled that sucker in like a champion.

• • •

Ian watched Pauly reel in her third fish of the day. This time, she grabbed it like a pro and wrestled the hook from its mouth without so much as a glance in his direction.

He whistled. "I didn't think you had it in you."

"Not surprised. You've spent the last three seasons underestimating me." She held up the hearty walleye and eyed Ian pointedly.

"We underestimated each other."

"Fair enough." She dropped the fish into the cooler and wiped her hands on the back of her jeans. "But from now on, we're going to encourage and support each other."

He laughed. "Are we gonna do trust falls now?"

"Everything's a big old joke to you, isn't it?"

"Not everything. I'm real serious about beer."

She rolled her eyes. "Why do you do that?"

"Do what?"

"Act like you don't care."

He shrugged. "Maybe I don't."

He didn't like the way she was staring at him. *Through* him. Like there was something vulnerable inside of him she could actually see. He should've kept his mouth shut about his mother.

"We should get back to the cabin so I still have some sunlight to clean by." He bent for the nearest rod and the soft-sided cooler.

"Okay. We can talk about the bottom of Charleston's lineup while we walk."

Oh, joy. Ian looped the cooler's strap over his head and across his body, then he reached for the handle of the hard-sided cooler that contained the fish packed in water and ice. "Knock yourself out," he said, taking off ahead of her, needing some space.

"Krisinski is their switch-hitter," she said when she caught up to him.

"And the guy only switches when the moon is full and the tide is high."

"Really? Where did you … Wait. You're messing with me."

"You gotta admit it's funny you thought it was possible even for a second. I mean, there's reasonable, and then there's obsessive. You're obsessive, Byrne."

She made a few noises in the back of her throat that sounded a little like posturing, but then she fell behind him without another word, probably to consider the validity of what he'd said.

With distance between them, Ian stopped thinking about Pauly long enough to get a tune stuck in his head. He whistled as he walked. Beneath the shade of the trees, the temperature was cooler, and he breathed freely and deeply. By sunset, it would be the perfect temperature for a fire. He would drag the Adirondack chairs off the porch, bust out his harmonica, and gladly waste time beneath the stars. He loved this place.

As he closed in on the back door to the cabin, the distinct sound of wheels on gravel stopped him.

"The guys?" Pauly asked.

Something didn't feel right. "Not unless the boat sank or Kenny Chesney canceled. Maybe my dad. I invited him, but he said he couldn't come."

When he rounded the corner of the house with Pauly at his side, he heard the crunching gravel again and caught a glimpse of a brown sedan and taillights.

"They must've thought nobody was home," she said. "Should we flag them down?"

He grabbed her wrist as it raised. "No." The hairs on the back of his neck stood. "I don't recognize that car. Probably made a wrong turn. It happens sometimes." But he couldn't shake the worried feeling.

"Are you ever scared to be way out here without a phone?"

Not usually.

He realized his hand was still wrapped around her wrist, so he released her. "I'm going to clean the fish. If you're squeamish, you'll want to go inside."

"Yep. That's where I draw the line."

Pauly headed for the house, and Ian tried not to think about the unexpected visitor. Instead, he piled everything he'd been carrying alongside the cabin and set his sights on the cleaning station he'd helped his father build with PVC piping and a garden hose. Back when his dad had come here on a regular basis. How long had that been? Six months? A year?

"Pratt?" Pauly's voice rose about the woodsy sounds. "You should come see this."

His worry magnified.

He jogged to the porch, where he found her pointing at a neon orange sign stuck to the front door. *Sheriff's Sale* was in bold letters across the top. "What?"

He leaned in and read every word, despite worry and anger blurring his vision the more he read. This property was going up for sheriff's sale. In forty-five days. "What the actual fuck?"

No wonder his father needed money. "First the car, now this!"

"Can I do anything to help?" Pauly stood with her butt resting against the railing. A look of concern wrinkled her face. She was looking at him like that again. Like the man she saw was someone vulnerable, someone who might break, someone who cared a hell of a lot more than he let on.

And maybe he was, maybe he did, because he dropped all pretense of being a happy-go-lucky guy and drove his fist into the notice, rattling the door. It took only a second for the pain to reach his brain. *Should've had more beer.*

"Pratt!" She ran to him. "What are you doing?" She grabbed his hand before he unleashed another punch. "That's your throwing hand."

He didn't care. In forty-five days, some son of a bitch would waltz in here and rip this place out from underneath him. Maybe it would be the same son of a bitch who bought the Thunderbird. His poor mom. Would she never be at peace?

"Hey." Pauly was closer now, so close he felt her breath on his cheek, spreading over his skin like balm. "Let me help you."

She could. If he kissed her, he could lose himself in those full lips and that wet mouth. He would feel something more than the ugliness tearing apart his insides.

Before he could make a move, though, she pulled him into the house and deposited him in his father's armchair. He slumped with his head back, his eyes closed, and his hand throbbing. Even if they won the championship, five grand wasn't enough to stop something like this from happening. *Fuck.*

The beer made him too groggy and foggy to consider alternatives, so he laid there, limp, listening to Pauly move around the cabin. Opening and closing cupboards and the fridge. Filling a water glass. Eventually, he sensed her at his side again.

"Take this," she said.

When he lifted his head and opened his eyes, he saw her open palm holding some pills.

"Ibuprofen," she said. "I don't leave home without it." A glass of water was in her other hand.

"Thanks." His voice was raw, and he welcomed the water. Metal flavor and all.

While he drank, she headed back to the kitchen and returned with an ancient bag of frozen peas. "Let me see that hand."

He made a few stiff fists. "It's fine."

"Don't be a hard-ass." She lifted his wrist and smoothed her thumb over the reddened knuckles.

He about jumped out of his skin, but not because it hurt. "You don't have to do this," he said gruffly.

"Yeah, I do. We can't win a championship if you're on the DL." She set his hand on his thigh and set the pack of peas on his hand. "Twenty minutes on. Twenty minutes off. Got it?"

"Got it." Wishing he'd kept it together out there, he let his head fall back again so he could avoid her knowing eyes and the probing questions that were probably lining up in her head.

A few minutes of silence passed, and then she asked, "Does this have anything to do with what I overheard at Foley's? About the money and the car?"

He exhaled, wanting to ignore her. But she'd scooped him up and saved his hand from another blow, and for that, she probably deserved an explanation. "I guess. My dad said he's trying to sell my mother's Thunderbird because he's behind on some bills, but I never thought it had anything to do with the cabin."

"There has to be somebody he can call to restructure payments."

You would think, but Ray Pratt didn't have a lot of gumption. "What if it's too late for that?"

"Pratt, look at me." Pauly pushed off the couch and landed on her knees beside him, one hand hot on his thigh. "I don't know how much your dad owes, but five grand is a good chunk of money.

It's someplace to start. So, we're going to win this championship, and you're going to help your dad. Got it?"

Short, staccato exhales relieved some of the pressure building in his chest. Why did she have to be so damn pretty? Why couldn't he look at her and see nothing but a teammate? He held her gaze and imagined meeting her in some bar, making her laugh, taking her home, making her moan. And just like that, all the pain in his hand, his heart, and his head evaporated.

"Okay"—she scrambled to her feet like she'd been burned—"I'll give you some space. When you're done icing, you should drive up to where you get reception and call your dad. Make sure he knows what's going on. And don't worry about me. I'll just study my reports for a while." She backed away but stopped. "Is there a specific room you want me in?"

Mine. He bit his cheek until it bled. "First one on your left." That way, she'd be far from where he'd be, all the way upstairs in the loft.

"Great. If you need me …" She pointed to the hallway.

He nodded, but he had no intention of bothering her—or his father. The porch and a couple more beers sounded like the better bet.

Chapter Five

The next morning, Pauly awoke feeling unrested and unsettled. The cabin was washed in sunlight but eerily quiet. She'd fallen asleep atop an ugly, slightly musty quilt, with her laptop in sleep mode by her side. In the tiny bathroom across the hall, she brushed her teeth and unwrapped her hair, which had been gathered beneath a silky scarf, and then she went off in search of Ian.

She found him in an Adirondack chair on the front porch, along with a dozen or so empty beer bottles. They were lined up on the railing and scattered around the floorboards. He looked hellish.

He glanced at her and grunted.

"Oh my God," she said. "Have you been out here all night?"

His red-rimmed eyes blinked as if they were trying to make sense of the situation, too. "Breakfast of champions." His scratchy voice rose at the end, making it sound like a question.

She rolled her eyes. "I don't see any champions here. Not yet. Not ever, if we don't get our shit together and work for it."

"I know." He actually sounded remorseful. Then again, maybe that was his usual hungover voice. "This isn't what it looks like."

"So you didn't drink two six packs and pass out on the porch?"

"No. I did that. I just don't do it often. Or ever, really. I usually know when to turn it off." He shoved a hand through his unruly hair and exhaled loudly. "That notice really messed me up."

The weight of his predicament wasn't lost on her, and she gave him an understanding nod. "But there are better ways to handle things. Did you call your dad?"

His expression soured. "No. If you think I look bad, he's probably ten times worse. I wasn't going to call and attempt a conversation with a drunk guy. I'll talk to him when I get home."

Maybe he would. But maybe he was stalling, too. That fit his personality. Avoid the serious stuff. Bury it under stupid jokes and a tidal wave of alcohol. That was a big character flaw. There might be an even bigger one, though. And she didn't need another catcher scratched at the last minute because of a substance abuse problem.

"Pratt—"

"I'm sorry." He pushed out of the chair and started to clean up. "The beers probably hit me harder than usual because we didn't get a chance to eat." He pointed across the yard to the toppled cooler. "Something sure had a field day. Raccoons or a bear." He laughed, like it was no big deal.

"And you were passed out on the front porch with wild animals sniffing around?" She leveled him with a look of concern. "I don't think not eating is the problem here."

His eyes narrowed, and then he turned his back on her, heading down the steps toward the garbage cans stored in fencing several yards from the house.

She didn't want to get too involved in his personal life and problems beyond what would produce results on the field. The facts were, Pratt was the starting catcher, and the Aces were headed to Charleston, West Virginia, in three days. If she didn't act fast, she could lose Pratt and any progress they'd made to the chaos in his personal life. And this late in the season, if she lost another starting catcher, she might as well kiss the championship goodbye.

There had to be a way to get through to him, to make these last few weeks matter to him as much as they mattered to her. But short of threatening him, she didn't know what to do. Unless … he would take a bribe.

"Hey!" she called out.

He turned.

"How would you like to double your money?"

"What are you talking about, Byrne?"

She followed him, cradling a half dozen empties in her arms. "Your championship bonus is five thousand dollars, so is mine. If you stay away from alcohol for the rest of the season, I'll sign over my bonus to you. That'll be ten grand."

His eyes turned cold, and his chin lifted. "I *don't* have a drinking problem."

"Then this'll be easy. Ten grand. Think about it. You can do a lot to help your dad with that." She squirmed on the inside but powered through. "Maybe you can even keep this place off the auction block." *Ick.* She was helping him, but she was exploiting him, too. That wasn't as underhanded as it seemed, was it?

He looked off into the distance somewhere beyond the house, his expression pinched. He seemed to be struggling, and she almost withdrew her offer and gave him an apology in its place. But then he said, "Fine," his tone dry. "You got yourself a deal."

She let out a huge breath and smiled.

His gaze shifted back to her, and he caught her relief, leveling her with a table-turning glare. "Why do you want this championship bad enough to give up five grand to get it?"

She hesitated. A sense of desperation nipped at her heels even as she said nonchalantly, "Just another feather in my cap."

"That's an expensive feather." He stared at her until he was staring through her, or maybe into her, judging by the feel of her skin crawling off her bones. "And I'm not buying it, Byrne. I changed my mind. No deal unless you tell me what's really going on here."

Could she risk opening up to Ian Pratt? Letting him in? Telling him about how badly she wanted to make it to the minors? Telling him about Holymount? Telling him about the fear she felt every time she thought about life after baseball? Maybe he deserved to know some of it. After all, she knew more about him than she'd ever wanted to know. It might even level the playing field.

But when she opened her mouth, she couldn't make the words come out.

Pauly looked down at the beer cans pressed against her empty stomach. "I can't think straight when I'm hungry."

When she met his gaze again, he rolled his eyes. "You're full of shit."

"I'm serious. I saw a few edible-looking things in the cupboards. How 'bout I cook us some breakfast, and then we can talk?"

He nodded slowly, never taking his prying eyes off her face. "Fine. But I'm holding you to it. Food first. Then you spill."

How had she ended up being the target?

• • •

Rather than hover over her in the kitchen, poking and prodding and waiting for her to come clean, Ian showered and erased the stink from yesterday. Hitting rock bottom was a lot easier to do when you were alone. Now, he knew why his dad was always pushing him away.

When he was done in the bathroom, Ian joined her in the kitchen, taking a seat at the table, where she'd set a plate of fried potatoes and a bowl of mixed beans. She'd even managed coffee somehow, when he didn't have a coffee maker.

"I'm impressed," he said.

"I'm the youngest of three, and I've been baseball poor for way too long. I know my way around canned goods." She pointed to the bowl. "Bean salad with oil and vinegar." She pointed to the plate. "White potatoes fried in butter and salted." And then to the mug that read: *You should've seen the one that got away.* "Coffee made in a saucepan. Watch out for the grounds. I tried to ladle around them but failed miserably."

He grinned. He'd never met anyone like her, not someone with so much … stick-with-it-ness. After his outburst and subsequent collapse, most people would've written him off and hightailed it outta here. But Pauly Byrne wasn't most people. She was determined to win that championship.

Ian ignored the impulse to ask her why, instead giving in to his watering mouth and grumbling stomach. He dug into the potatoes. Dark and crispy at the edges, soft and buttery in the middle. "Damn," he said around a mouthful. "This is freaking gourmet."

She snorted a laugh. "That's because you're hungover, and you haven't eaten since yesterday. You want gourmet, ask Caceres to cook for you. He made me rice and enchiladas from scratch once." Her eyes rolled back, and a sexy moan caught in her throat. "Amazing."

That sound and the mention of the Aces' center fielder created a surge of jealousy. Ian studied the strong lines of her face and her smooth, dark skin, and wondered if Caceres had noticed how beautiful she was, too. Made her a meal. Made a few moves. The guy might be spoken for now, but he used to be hella smooth.

"What?" she asked, her face bunched in question, her eyes trained on him like she knew what he was thinking.

"Nothing," he said, trying to sound cool. "I was just imagining you and Caceres sharing a meal."

"Helen Anne and her daughter were there, too. In fact, I was being a role model to Macy."

"Oh. Okay. I thought maybe …" He swallowed the words with a mouthful of beans.

"Maybe what?" Her tone was clipped.

"Never mind."

"Don't be an idiot, Pratt. I take baseball way too seriously to look at a teammate sideways." Funny, she looked away from him right quick.

"So you've never even thought a teammate was good-looking?"

She kept her eyes on her plate. "I like guys who aren't athletes."

Sounded like she was evading. "Like what? Artists? Musicians?"

"Nope." She shut him down with a shake of the head.

A sore spot.

"I'm here to talk baseball not *boys*," she said, her eyes narrowed. "If Rialis comes to the plate with runners on, what are you going to call?"

"I don't know. I'll tell you when he comes to the plate with runners on."

She ignored his casual response and charged ahead. "He usually goes deep into the pitch count. He can see the junk." Deep vertical lines formed in the skin between her brows.

"And that worries you?"

"Of course. If he can see what I'm throwing, and he sits back, I'm screwed."

Ian pretended to think about that long and hard, stroking his thumb and forefinger in a V shape along his chin. "But what if his vision is blurry for some reason?" A healthy dose of melodrama infused his voice. "What if he forgets to clean his contacts or gets something in his eyes? What if he has allergies?"

"You're such a smart-ass," she said. "We'll see how hard you're laughing if we don't make it past Charleston."

He probably wouldn't be laughing. That ten grand could definitely come in handy. Ian gulped down the hot coffee, grounds and all. Having something other than beer in his belly made him feel alive again.

"I would call a fastball straight down the pipe," he said. "Rialis isn't a power hitter. Give him something he can hit, and trust your fielders."

Her lips parted, and she nodded slowly, like she was considering it. Then she shook him off like she'd done way too many times on the mound. "I don't like leaving my fate in someone else's hands. I would rather strike him out."

"Suit yourself." Ian took another bite of beans. "But it's called a team for a reason." He rested his fork on the edge of his plate and smiled at her after he swallowed. "Now, tell me why you want to win a championship so badly."

She broke eye contact.

"Come on, Byrne. You've had a front-row seat to my shit show. Give me some dirt on you."

"It's not that dramatic. I just want to win because I like to win." When he raised his brows, she added, "And because that's the only way left for me to attract attention and get my contract bought out."

"Okay. I'll buy that." But her posture was still rigid, and she went back to being literally tight-lipped. "What else aren't you telling me?"

"Nothing," she said, looking away again.

"Byrne, I'm going to bug the shit out of you until you fess up."

"You're annoying as hell."

"I'll take that as a compliment." He grinned. "Now, come on. Give it to me. The more we know about what motivates the other, the better off we'll be."

She caved with a noisy exhale. "The bottom line is I don't want to think about life after baseball. Winning a championship and making it to the minors would delay that. But I probably need to think about it either way, because I only have one more year of Independence League eligibility after this season. What if something fluky happens and we don't win? What if I don't make it any higher? Then what?"

"You can play sandlot with me," he said, not at all surprised when she rolled her eyes. "What about international leagues?"

"Short seasons. Shitty pay."

"Money isn't everything."

"It is when your parents have been working five jobs between them for the last seventeen years to support your dreams. They need a break. Shoot, they need to have their own dreams."

"So what are your options?"

"I could go back to school for my teaching certification, get a real job, find a coaching position somewhere." Her mouth twisted. "In fact, Holymount University, where I went to college, is looking for a pitching coach right now."

He nodded. She was wrestling with some heavy thoughts. "Are you going to apply?"

"I'm thinking about it. For my parents' sake. But it would shorten my playing days by an entire season, and that stinks."

It did. She might not be his favorite person on the planet, but she was talented, and he didn't want to see her cut her career short, either. "Well, I don't think you have a choice then."

She met his gaze with wide eyes. "Really?"

"We need to work our asses off these next few weeks and get you noticed by the big leagues. Then you won't have to worry about life after baseball."

Her eyes never left his, which was how he saw them brighten until they sparkled. "Thank you for saying that."

"Thank you for saving my throwing hand," he said, showing off his lightly bruised and battered knuckles. "*Now*, we're even."

"Yep, and we have a deal. Right?" Her brows raised.

"I don't know."

"I followed through. I told you why the championship is so important to me. Now, it's your turn. I'll give you my signing bonus if you stop drinking for the rest of the season."

"I *don't* have a drinking problem," he said, but he did need the money. With a grin, he added, "Kiss your five Gs goodbye, Byrne."

"We gotta win first."

"Piece of cake."

"How do you know?"

"I've seen our pitcher in action. She doesn't give up."

He was laying it on a little thick, but that didn't mean he didn't believe it.

Better yet, she looked like she believed it, too.

•••

Pauly bent over and tied her running shoes. "What would Coach say if he knew we were going to toss without doing a few warmup laps?" Out of the corner of her eye, she could see Pratt leaning against the porch railing. There'd never been a man who'd looked more comfortable in a T-shirt and court shorts. And sexy. *Don't forget sexy.* She wrinkled her nose and chased that thought from her mind.

"Who says we aren't warming up?" Pratt jogged down the porch steps, calves and quads flexing.

"What are we gonna do? Run around the cabin?" Because she wasn't interested in turning an ankle while dodging potholes on what passed for the main road.

"There's a trail that runs along the river. We'll take it easy and enjoy the view."

Ten minutes later, Pauly was enjoying the wrong view, watching Pratt's rock-hard ass twitch beneath his shorts as he dashed ahead on an open patch of trail. What he didn't know couldn't hurt either of them, so she kept right on staring. If he caught her, she'd blame her behavior on decreased oxygen from the workout.

"Favorite team of all time?" he asked, ripping her out of her trance.

She bounced along the path behind him. "If we're talking franchise, then it's the Orioles. A Baltimore girl's gotta represent. Specific team, though? I'd say the 2004 Red Sox."

Pratt whistled. "That was a good series. Unless you were a Cards fan." His laughter carried on the warm wind.

Huh. Pratt knew the 2004 World Series participants offhand? Aside from her dad, she'd never met a man who could match her skill for baseball trivia.

Up ahead, the trail narrowed, filling in with leafy branches and jagged sticks. Pratt slowed his pace until Pauly was almost on top of him.

She pulled back—way back. "How 'bout you?"

"I was all over the place. If a team was hot, I was a diehard fan."

"Bandwagoner."

"Yep. I was more into individual players than teams."

"Like who?"

"Big Unit, baby. I used to dream of catching for Randy Johnson."

Pauly tripped and grabbed a tree to stop herself from tumbling forward. "Are you serious?"

"Yeah, why?" He glanced behind him and gave her a little smirk, one that said he'd somehow seen or sensed her stumble.

She was too rattled by his admission to be embarrassed. "Johnson's *my* favorite player. I used to dream of pitching like him. I still wear his T-shirt jersey to bed the night before I pitch."

The trail widened again, and they ran side by side.

"Well, shit," Pratt said, eyes shining.

Damn, he was a good-looking man.

"Is that why you favor your slider?" he asked.

"Maybe. I've never thought about it. I just like the way the slider feels. Setting up off-center and then snapping my wrist." She mocked the motion with her hand and smiled. "It gives me power I don't get with my fastball. And I *love* power."

He chuckled and nudged her with his elbow before he picked up his pace. "It would really suck if you quit playing, Byrne."

She opened her mouth to say he didn't have to worry about that, that they could work together to keep her in baseball as long as possible, but she closed it without saying a word. He didn't *really* care where she ended up next year or the year after that. He was just being friendly and supportive amid playoffs, treating her like a teammate, like he should've been treating her all along. She wasn't going to make more out of it.

"I'm going to start calling you Big Unit," he said.

She laughed. "Don't."

"Why? I have nicknames for everybody."

"Big Unit sounds …" She paused for a breath. "Weird."

"Because it sounds like I'm saying you have a big dick?"

"Yep."

"Well, you do. Figuratively speaking. And that's a compliment."

She appreciated that, but she still didn't want him calling her Big Unit, so she circled back to the topic that started it all. "I can't believe we have the same favorite player."

"Wonder what else we have in common." He slid a glance in her direction and picked up his pace.

She matched him, step for step.

"Who else do you like?" he asked. "Player-wise."

"Jeter." Talking was a little harder now. Her heart was pumping. Her body was loose and warm. A sense of calm settled over her, and she smiled. "Gotta love Jeter. Consistent and classy."

"Top five here, too. Probably top three. Who else?"

"Maddux. Gotta love a pitcher whose brain works like an encyclopedia of batters—just like mine."

Pratt rolled his eyes, but he laughed.

Eventually, the route dipped to the water, and they turned around, embroiled in a passionate discussion about where Albert Pujols and Miguel Cabrera fit on their lists.

"It's not even a contest," Pratt said. "Pujols is one of the greatest hitters of all time."

"Miggy's got power, a great strikeout percentage, and a walk rate that's scary."

"Then it's a tie. Al and Miggy at four." Pratt lifted his hand palm up, and she met him midair. A smack and a tingle. The contact was over in seconds, but the heat from his hand went straight to her cheeks.

Her breath came in staccato bursts along with an undeniable awareness. *Damn it.* She liked him. Not the teammate. Not the party-guy persona. The actual man who inhabited a mouthwatering outer layer. The man who taught her to fish, missed his mother, and talked baseball like Pauly did. For the first time since Tyler had dropped her flat, she wanted a man in her life. That was the only part about life after baseball she didn't mind thinking about. A real relationship. Falling in love. Having someone in her corner. Always. Maybe when she got back to Arlington, she would get a head start on it, give Flynn her specs. Tall and built, with a brain capable of spouting baseball trivia. How hard could it be to find someone like that who wasn't her teammate?

She must've been projecting those thoughts onto Ian, because his smile faltered and he picked up his pace. "Less talking, more running," he said.

So they ran, and Pauly tried not to think about how much she enjoyed his company and their peaceful surroundings. She trained her mind on baseball facts again and pushed herself until she could tell by her breathing she was in her target heart rate zone.

After a few minutes, Pratt said, "Now it's too damn quiet. I need music." He pointed to his ears. "What do you listen to when you run?"

"My thoughts," she answered honestly.

He slowed down and glanced at her. "You never listen to music when you're working out?"

She shook her head.

"Who's your favorite artist?" he asked.

"Don't have one."

"Last concert you went to?"

"Never been to one."

He looked at her funny.

"I'm not really into music," she said, exhaling every so many words. "I like to keep my brain quiet and focused on baseball."

"Damn, Byrne," he said with a breathy chuckle. "You're wound tighter than anyone I know."

It was true, and Pratt wasn't the first guy to point that out. She fell behind him a few more steps, frowning. The sorry truth was, Flynn could look all he wanted, but he wasn't going to find a guy who appreciated the tightly wound part of her.

"I'll race you back," Pratt said. "Loser has to chase the balls."

Pauly took off running before she said, "Deal."

Chapter Six

Ian caught up with Pauly on the side lawn. She was breathless and bent at the waist, gripping her knees, peering at him from beneath a waterfall of curly hair. "I won," she said matter-of-factly.

He blinked and imagined tackling her, rolling around in the grass, kissing her until their breath returned to normal. But she was way too damn focused on baseball to be interested in a little fun with a guy like him.

He bent over, too, opening his mouth to breathe. "You cheat," he managed.

"No way. I saw an advantage, and I took it. We never established rules." She straightened and stretched her arms above her head, lifting her face to the rays of sun that broke through the trees. Her T-shirt inched higher on her stomach until a line of smooth, dark skin appeared.

Ian dropped his head and stared at his feet, willing the blood to redirect. He usually ignored rules if it meant having fun, but having fun could get him into serious trouble out here. Maybe if he came clean about what he was thinking, she would put him in his place. She was good at that.

"Pauly," he said, standing and taking one more fortifying breath.

Shock riddled her face, and then she laughed. "You called me by my first name."

"I did?"

"You did. It sounded weird."

But it felt right. Byrne didn't fit anymore. "Pauly," he said again, testing it out, his voice lower and softer this time.

Her expression morphed into something more serious, but she didn't break eye contact. "Does this mean I get to call you Ian?"

He smiled at the sound of his name on her lips. "Absolutely."

"Okay." She said it slowly, like she wasn't sure.

"Because we're more than teammates now," he said carefully. "We're friends."

She nodded. Still serious. Still locked in an intense staring match.

"And as your friend," he said, "I gotta tell you something." He walked toward her, and she didn't even blink. "It isn't nice to cheat."

She laughed and drilled her fisted hands into his chest. "I didn't cheat. I just got a head start."

"Same difference," he said, grabbing her hands by the wrists and holding them out to the sides of her body.

She squirmed against his grip, her eyes flashing over his face, her lips parted in disbelief. "Fine. We'll go again. No head starts this time."

He barely resisted the urge to haul her against him and released her instead.

"I'm still going to win," she said, backpedaling out of his reach, laughing as she went.

"Oh, yeah?" He took off after her, not exactly sure he could keep things "friendly" when he caught her.

She rounded the cabin a few beats before he did, and her shriek echoed in the summer breeze.

"Hey! Is everything—" Ian came face to face with his dad.

Ray sat in an Adirondack chair on the front porch with a beer in hand.

"Shit," Ian said under his breath, and then he called out a little louder, "Hey, Dad."

The old man nodded and tipped his head in Pauly's direction.

"Hi," she said. Then she looked at Ian. "You guys have a lot to talk about. I should go."

Ian reached for her in a burst of panic, catching her by the hand. "No." He dropped the limb almost as soon as he'd grabbed it. "We still have work to do. Go take a shower or something. I'll figure this out."

She pursed her lips and seemed to think about it. "Okay, but seriously, I don't want to be in the way."

He wanted her in the way. Otherwise, there'd be nothing stopping him from joining his dad in dead space, where there'd be too much beer and too little talking.

Ray eyed them carefully as they climbed the steps. "Sorry if I'm interruptin'," he said, looking like he hadn't showered in days.

Pinpricks of embarrassment heated Ian's face.

"Hi, Mr. Pratt." Pauly went to him, her hand outstretched. "I'm Pauly Byrne. Nice to formally meet you. I'm gonna go inside and get out of your way." She rushed Ian a sympathetic but encouraging look before she disappeared into the house.

The connection and calm they'd cultivated in the woods was gone, leaving him alone and jittery. Maybe he should've let her go, too. Been a man. Faced this head-on. But the Pratt men had never been very good at that.

"Dad." Ian leaned against the railing. "What are you doing here?"

Ray swallowed a mouthful of beer and snorted. "Whaddya mean what am I doin' here? I own the place."

Ian let that last bit slide for a minute, because he was more concerned about the slurred words. "You drove like this?"

"Course I drove. I sure as hell didn't walk."

"*Jesus*, Dad. That's stupid dangerous. You're drunk."

"Am not. And don't you lecture me, boy. I made it, didn't I? Not a scratch on the car."

"Doesn't make it okay, and you're not getting back in that car until you're sober."

"You're just pissed I ruined your romantic weekend."

Ian's jaw clenched. "She's not my girl. She's my pitcher. But, yeah. You showing up like this kinda puts a damper on things."

Ray grunted again. "Well, excuse me for wantin' to warn you 'bout the sheriff."

Between the slurring and the holes in the sentence, Ian would've been lost if he hadn't seen the notice.

"Already been here," he said. "They posted a pretty orange sign on the door yesterday. Don't you think you should've told me this was a possibility sooner?"

Ray shrugged, like it was no big deal. "I'd rather see you havin' fun than worryin' about this shit."

And he'd rather be having fun, but he couldn't ignore what was going on any longer. "First the car. Now the camp. Dad, what the hell is going on?"

"Where's your beer?" Ray asked, ignoring Ian's question and raising his can to his mouth.

Ian wanted one. He couldn't imagine getting through the next twenty-four hours alongside this man without something to smooth the rough edges. But he'd made a promise to Pauly, and he intended to keep it—if for no other reason than to prove he didn't have a drinking problem.

"I'm off the sauce until after the season," Ian said.

Ray's face soured, and his head bobbled from all the liquor swimming around in it. "Better you than me."

Ian looked away. What now? He wanted to help, but he wasn't good in critical situations. He liked taking the easy way out. Unfortunately, he couldn't see an easy way out of this. But he thought of Pauly, showering in peace, expecting him to be out here making headway with his dad, and he decided to try being that guy for a minute.

"How much do you need to keep this camp from being sold?" he asked.

Ray's eyes drooped, and his head lolled to one side. He looked ready to pass out. If Ian hadn't seen it so many times before, he would've been alarmed.

"Lemme finish my beer in peace," Ray said.

The easy way. Ray would drink and drift off, and Ian would get a reprieve. He could tell Pauly Ray had passed out before they'd had a chance to discuss things. It wouldn't be a lie, really. But a niggle of something proactive wouldn't die.

"Is this a foreclosure?" Ian asked. "Is that what we're dealing with? Can we stop it?" So many questions, and the longer he stared at his drunken father without getting a response, the angrier he felt.

"Why the fuck do you care?" Ray finally snapped. "Never cared before."

Ian rushed to defend himself, but he couldn't. He cared. Of course, he cared, but he couldn't recall ever having helped his dad with anything specific. Other people always seemed worse off. His mom. His Aunt May. Friends like Mandy. Ray Pratt got by, often treating other people like shit. He handled things on his own—with a little boost from booze. And look where that had led. As much as Ian didn't want to lead this charge, this time, he didn't have a choice.

"Dad, we need to figure this out. For Mom's sake."

Ray shot him a withering look. "Leave her out of this."

"How can I? She's gonna lose her final resting place if her husband doesn't step up and fix whatever mess he's made."

Ray threw the beer can, and Ian ducked before it collided with his head. In shock, he straightened.

"Don't attack me," Ray slurred. "I did my best."

Maybe so. But it wasn't enough.

Ian propped his elbow on his folded arm and raised his knuckles to his mouth. *What now?*

"Get me another beer," Ray said, his eyes closed and his head leaning back against the chair.

And Ian folded, because it was easier than standing out here, having a dead-end conversation.

Right now, it needed to be enough to have one Pratt sober.

• • •

Pauly heard the screen door slam and assumed it was Ian. The steps that followed were too heavy and too sure to come from the obviously inebriated man she'd met on the porch.

"I can't find towels," she called down the hall, having already checked underneath the bathroom vanity.

"In the closet in my dad's room. Across the hall from where you stayed." Ian sounded gruff, like things weren't going well out on the porch.

She hesitated, wondering if she could help, but when it came to Ian, it was safer for her to stay out of the way, out of anything that didn't have to do with baseball.

In the room across the hall, she found sheets and blankets on the top two closet shelves, and then finally towels at knee height. She squatted, grabbed one, and rooted around for a washcloth. Her hand brushed something jagged but flexible. Paper of some kind. A stack of it. Her fingertips met resistance on a glossy surface. Photographs. Curiosity got the better of her, and she stilled, listening for Ian. When she didn't hear any more noises coming from the front of the cabin, she pulled the pile from the shelf and flipped through.

A bucktoothed and wild-haired kid with Ian's sharp blue eyes sat on the dock, a can of Coke between his skinny knees. She smiled at the photograph and flipped to the next one. The same little boy on the dock with his back to the camera. A woman leaned over him and planted a kiss on the top of his head. His right hand was raised in what looked like an effort to get her to leave. Pauly couldn't see much of the woman's face, but she could tell the woman was smiling.

There were more pictures of the woman, pictures that captured a strong resemblance to Ian. The same off-kilter smile. Flashy at first glance, but missing something when you studied it. And as happy as the photos seemed, they made Pauly sad … and guilty for intruding.

She gathered them up to put them away, and a tri-folded letter slipped from the pile. Loopy handwriting bled through the paper, and again, curiosity got the better of her.

May 18, 2002

Hey, Buddy. I'm lying on my cot thinking about you. I know you're getting ready for school to end and you'll be packing up and heading to camp soon. I wish I could be there, but we're making real progress. The bad guys are being pushed back farther each day. Hopefully, they'll be out of Afghanistan soon, and I'll be home with you before the summer is over. Be good. Fish a lot. Play some baseball. Most of all, have fun! Knowing you're home laughing and playing is all I need to get through. Write me when you can. I miss you. I love you!! Everything I do is to make the world a safer place, so you can grow up happy.

Hugs and kisses (don't wipe them off!),

Mom

"What are you doing?"

Pauly startled at the sound of Ian's voice. She reared up and smacked a stray tear off her cheek just as he crossed the room and ripped the pile of personal items out of her hands.

"I'm sorry, I—"

"Can't mind your own business?"

"No. I found that stuff when I was looking for a towel."

"And you just *had* to examine it?" He laughed humorlessly. "So much for your famous control."

She straightened in defense. "Why's it such a big deal? They're happy pictures, and the letter was sweet."

Instead of answering, he left the room, taking the pile with him.

Pauly stood there a beat, stunned and confused, before she took off after him. "Ian, wait. I'm sorry. I shouldn't have read the letter, but—"

He turned on her at the end of the hall just as his dad opened the front door and stumbled into the living area, filling the cabin with even more unwanted tension.

"S'wrong wit the satellite?" the man asked, a smart phone in hand.

Ian's anger over finding her with the mementos morphed into something shifty. "I don't know." He rushed toward the door, where his father swayed unsteadily. "We'll look later."

"Tryin' to check email," Mr. Pratt said.

"Email?" Pauly stared at Ian. "I thought you didn't have Wi-Fi."

"Satellite," his father said, steadying himself with a nearby chair. "Sucks."

Ian closed his eyes briefly and shook his head. "We have satellite internet," he clarified. "I told you we didn't because I just wanted some peace. I still just want some peace. You barged in with all these plans to study reports and call Skip, and I just wanted …" He looked at the stack of photos in his hands. "I'm sorry."

She glared at him. She wanted to be mad. She had a right to be mad. But in the middle of all this chaos, she couldn't sustain it enough to attack him like he'd attacked her.

"Then we're even," she said, looking pointedly at the pictures.

He nodded.

"Good, then I'm going to get my stuff and go home." She made it halfway down the hall before a loud thud turned her around.

Ian's dad had collapsed. When she got closer, she realized he'd passed out, and by the frustrated but unfazed expression on Ian's face, it wasn't the first time something like this had happened.

"Should we call an ambulance?" she asked.

"He's drunk. He's not dying." Ian sounded disgusted, but he looked sad.

"Here," she said, reaching for one of the man's bony arms. "I'll help you get him to the couch."

Ian tried to shake her off, but she stood her ground.

When they had Mr. Pratt resting comfortably, Ian faced her. "You can go." His voice was flat. "I'll keep an eye on him."

But she could've sworn his eyes were begging her to stay. This was a lot for one person to handle. And three days before the divisional playoffs?

"I don't know," she said. "I'd feel better hanging around. That way, if you need an ambulance, I can drive up the hill to make the call while you stay back here with him."

Ian managed a sad smile. "You never give up, Byrne. Do you?"

"Not usually."

"I appreciate the offer, but I can't ask you to stay. It's too much."

"You're not asking me. I'm telling you. I'm staying."

There was more than a championship at stake here.

Chapter Seven

Hours passed with Pauly sitting at the dining table. At some point, she'd fallen into an online rabbit hole of information about foreclosures and sheriff's auctions. "The devil is in the details," her father liked to say, and Pauly thrived on the time and energy it took to unravel complicated situations. That was why she loved pitching. She didn't often get to apply those skills to non-baseball things, so maybe that was why she was still here. For the challenge.

She glanced at the couch, where Mr. Pratt snored. He'd been up a couple times in search of more beer, but Ian had insisted on water. Now, the sun was low in the sky, and the weather had turned unseasonably chilly.

The door latch clattered, and Ian pushed into the cabin with the strength of his back. His arm muscles contracted around a decent-sized pile of wood. He kicked the door closed and looked at the sofa and then at her.

Pauly smiled and lowered her eyes to the computer screen. They didn't stay there, though. They wandered back up and over to Ian, who squatted beside the stone hearth.

He'd changed since their workout. Now, a thin T-shirt pulled across his back as he stacked logs inside the firebox, and loose jeans rode low on his hips, revealing the band of his boxer briefs. Her weight-room conversation with Flynn came to mind. She was definitely ogling now.

And with that, she went back to her Google search, stealing glances every so often.

Before long, the fire roared, casting a glow on his face, which was riddled with concentration. The spark in her chest burned a little hotter. She wished she could forget everything she'd learned about him over the past two days and go back to thinking he was just an asshole … or a dick … or a shallow party boy who didn't care about anything but getting drunk and lucky.

He walked toward her, and she tried like hell to look like she hadn't been watching or thinking about him.

"I'm sorry," he said, his voice soft and rumbly.

She stared at the screen. "You said that already. A few times."

"Because I mean it. This isn't what you came for."

"This isn't what you came for either."

"Fair enough."

"So we deal."

He sat, noiselessly sliding his chair closer to hers. "I appreciate it. I really do. Nobody's ever done anything like this for me."

"Nobody's ever helped you before?" She found that hard to believe. "You had to have a favorite teacher or coach. That's help."

"Yeah, but not like this. Telling me to drop my weight back is easy, but"—he tapped the edge of her computer screen—"hanging out with me and my drunk dad, researching sheriff's sales is heavy, and I don't do heavy. I sure as hell never expected anyone to do it with me."

She ignored the worrisome flutter in her chest and made a face. "Why don't you *do heavy*?"

He shrugged, and she expected him to sidestep, but a second later, his brow furrowed, and he said, "I don't know. It's just the way I am. I can't see how you can get messed up in something heavy without being dragged down by it."

For some reason, she thought about his mother and the letter she'd read, but she didn't dare mention it. "I think you're stronger than that."

The way he looked at her—really looked at her—littered goose pimples across her skin.

"Everybody's stronger than they think they are," she said, hoping to diffuse whatever weirdness she'd created.

He nodded. "Maybe. But seriously. Thank you."

"Like I said. It's not a big deal." She put a healthy dose of indifference into her voice. "I like to gather data and analyze things. That's all."

"That's all?"

"Well, that and if you're stressed out, then your head won't be in the game. I don't want a bunch of passed balls to cost us a championship."

He snorted, half laugh, half challenge. "You shouldn't be worrying about my balls."

And just like that, she wasn't thinking about baseballs anymore.

The fire crackled, and Mr. Pratt snored. Pauly looked at the drunk man on the couch and back to her computer screen. "I'm worried about a lot of things," she said honestly. "You've got your hands full, Pratt."

"With the wrong thing." But he'd said it so low beneath his breath, she wasn't sure she'd heard him correctly, and then he followed that up with a clearer question. "What happened to Ian?"

It took her a second to catch on. She'd called him Pratt. "Old habit."

"So we're still friends? All of this hasn't ruined that?"

"Of course not." She glanced at him.

"Good. Because I like being *friendly* with you." The corner of his lips quirked, and his pupils dilated. Not very friendly. Kind of hungry and intense. And the longer he looked at her, the more she felt it too. *Needy.* The buzz in her blood. The heat on her skin.

She slid to the far side of her chair, putting another inch between them. "So." She cleared her throat and pointed at the laptop screen. "Here's what I've come up with. These five attorneys claim to be able to stop 99.9 percent of foreclosures and property sales by working with creditors and, in extreme cases, by helping the debtor file bankruptcy and restructure their debt. They have good reviews and ratings. Nothing seems shady. I think your dad should contact one of them and have a professional in his corner before he calls the county."

Mr. Pratt's snores grew louder and more agitated before settling down and leveling out again.

Ian shook his head. "He's gonna need all the help he can get."

"That's why I checked on something else while you were outside." She took a breath and forged ahead. "Have you ever talked to him about hospital-based detox or rehab?"

Ian's posture went stiff. "He doesn't need rehab. He just needs to drink less." There was denial in his voice and not a lot of conviction behind his smile.

"I don't know if it's that simple."

"I do." He reached out and shut her laptop. "I know the man better than anyone else. He's a lot like me. We drink to pass the time and block out bad shit, but we can turn it off like that." He snapped his fingers soundlessly.

She looked at the man on the couch, balled up in a fetal position. Social drinkers weren't belligerent drunks. They didn't pass out regularly. "Ian—"

"Pauly." His hand landed on her thigh, igniting a path straight to her center. "I like when you call me Ian." His blue eyes turned smoke-gray as they scanned her face, landing soundly on her lips.

Her mouth watered. Her body liquidated. "I guess it's better than calling you asshole."

He grinned. "I like when you call me that, too. With fire in your eyes. It's ... sexy." He slid his hand higher, his fingers almost grazing the crease of her hip.

Man, it was hot in here. They didn't need that damn fire. She inhaled, hoping for clarity, and wrapped her hand around his wrist, fully expecting to drag his fingers away from ground zero.

But there was the stretch of her skin around his girth and the feel of his heart beating in her hand, and she liked the way it felt.

He leaned closer, until their exhales mingled.

Full-body tingles pushed her to the brink, but she didn't care. She wanted it. She deserved it. All these years. Always in control. Always playing by the rules.

"Pauly," Ian whispered, bringing his lips to within a breath of hers. "I'm going to kiss you now."

She shuddered on an exhale. "Okay." Her eyes drifted shut in preparation.

A heartbeat later, a loud snore shattered the mood, and then the sound of glass breaking brought them to their feet.

"Dad," Ian said.

The man waved an arm back and forth over the coffee table, mumbling about his beer, but he'd apparently connected with a water glass.

Ian went to him.

Pauly stayed at the table, clearheaded and shaken. Was she insane? She scrubbed the remnants of Ian's hot breath from her lips. Kissing her catcher? Dear God, that was a line she couldn't afford to cross.

While Ian helped his father into the bathroom, Pauly tried to decide what to do next. If she stayed, she was going to have to be clear with him. That kind of coziness couldn't happen again.

She didn't know how long she'd been sitting there, mindlessly staring at her computer screen, when she caught movement out of the corner of her eye. Ian was standing in the hallway, watching her. When she looked closer, she saw a serious expression on his face, and she suspected he'd had time to think and had regrets, too. But a moment later, he was back to his usual flashy smile. Evading.

"Where were we?" he asked, his voice dripping with suggestion.

"We were about to make a terrible mistake."

"Oh *really?*" He approached on languid limbs, eyes locked on a prize.

"Yes, really." She pushed back the chair and stood to face him. "Cut the crap, Pratt. It isn't going to happen."

"So I'm Pratt again?"

"Would you rather be asshole?"

He grinned, and she felt it in her core. How could you want to rip somebody apart at the exact same time you want to rip off their clothes and pin them beneath you?

"Don't think I don't know what's happening here," she said.

He chuckled, and the timbre vibrated in her chest. "What's happening here?"

"You're sober, and you're needy, so you're hitting on me because I'm the only woman around, and sex is easier than facing the truth about your dad." She took a breath and leveled him with a concerned expression. "He's an alcoholic, and he needs rehab."

Ian's eyes widened, and he barked a laugh. "That's *not* what's happening here."

She wasn't going to argue with someone who wasn't willing to admit he had a problem. "Well, whatever is happening here is putting our *friendship* at risk," she said.

"That's for damn sure. Friends don't want to do what I want to do to you."

She could read every tawdry detail on his face.

A growl of frustration—and something else—ripped from her chest. "All I want from you is a championship."

"I don't believe it. Five minutes ago, you said I could kiss you."

"Five minutes ago, I was temporarily insane."

He laughed, and she needed to put some space between them. Hit the reset button. Clear her head.

"I'm going to go now. If everything is okay here with your dad."

Ian kept looking at her like she was crazier than he was. "Everything's great."

She was surprised he didn't try to use his father to make her stay.

With his blessing, she broke away, gathered her things, and faced him again before she opened the door. "I wrote the names of the attorneys and"—she rushed a glance down the empty hall, not wanting Mr. Pratt to overhear—"another number on a notepad. It's on the table. I really hope you figure things out here."

Ian's gaze wandered over her. "Thank you," he said, sounding sincere, but the same glint of mischief shone in his eyes. "I'll see you at practice on Thursday." He grinned. "Unless I see you before then."

"You'll see me at practice." And the thought of that alone made her head spin.

"It should be fun."

After this, it was going to be a nightmare.

•••

Ian stared at the door where Pauly had been, still feeling the buzz of their interaction. She was wrong. What he felt for her was more than a welcome distraction from this mess with his dad.

Wasn't it?

"Where'd your girl go?"

Ian faced his father, who was using both walls at the end of the hallway to hold himself up. It wasn't worth correcting him.

"She had to get back to Arlington." Away from this shit show.

"Good. More beer for us."

Ian looked at the table, where she'd scrawled the attorneys' information on a Burt's Bait and Tackle notepad. There was a 1-800 number underlined with an asterisk at the bottom. How much did he want to bet that undefined number was for a hospital or rehab? He refused to believe his dad was that far gone.

"We're out of beer," Ian said, making a mental note to stash the remaining beer in the bed of his truck once his father had fallen asleep.

"We ain't out." Ray wobbled forward and caught himself on the table.

"I'll have to go into town and get some later." Which wasn't going to happen.

"Well, shit." Ray's face went slack and pale.

For a split second, Ian wondered if Pauly was right. But then he shut down the thought. Drinking wasn't a habit for either of them. It was a crutch. There was a difference, and he held on to that.

He grabbed the notepad and cleared his throat. "Dad, you need to sober up anyway. You have to make some phone calls."

"To who?"

"I have the name of some lawyers here who should be able to help keep the cabin off the auction block."

"I don't need no bloodsucking lawyers. I got no goddamned money to pay 'em."

"Dad, we gotta do something."

"Don't waste your time." Ray wobbled across the floor. "Go home. Find your girl. Have some fun." He stumbled out the front door and into the cold. "I'm going to stay right here and soak up the peace for as long as I can." The man settled in an Adirondack chair and promptly fell asleep.

Ian wanted to bail. He had his truck keys in hand already. But that annoying voice in the back of his head said bailing wouldn't fix things. He glanced at the pile of pictures on the kitchen counter and saw his mother's smiling face. As frustrating as this was, he couldn't face her again—if he should be so lucky—without putting up an honest fight.

He hooked his keys on the wood by the door and focused on the notepad. It was time to suck it up and get serious.

Using the technique Pauly had used earlier, Ian boiled some water and made coffee. Then he grabbed his phone and joined his father on the porch. He nudged the man until Ray woke and accepted the mug.

"We're going to do this whether you like it or not," Ian said.

Ray wrinkled his nose and sipped the black tar. Then he gagged. "*Jesus*, are you trying to kill me?"

"No. I'm trying to sober you up. I'm going to sit out here and call these lawyers, and you're going to stay beside me in case they have questions I can't answer."

Ray blinked. "But it's cold."

Which meant the alcohol was wearing off. "Then we can go back inside, but either way, we're doing this."

"You don't need to. It's not your problem."

"I want to," Ian said, thinking about Pauly saying something similar. "So deal with it."

An hour later, Ian had called every lawyer on the list. Some offices were closed for the night, but he'd managed to talk to one paralegal, who was full of information that may or may not pertain to his father's situation, and one attorney, who was leaving for the day but was willing to talk to him again. Ray, of course, had fallen asleep on the couch in front of the fire five minutes into Ian's first call. There was no resolution, but somehow, Ian felt … accomplished.

He found Pauly's contact info in his phone and opened a new text message. She'd had plenty of time to get from the camp to Arlington.

Ian: Are you home?

Three little dots flickered on his screen, letting him know she was typing. Those three little dots made him smile, but then they disappeared. He waited, preparing for her not to respond. She may have agreed to let him kiss her in the heat of the moment, but now, it was clear she was going to fight him every step of the way.

The dots reappeared.

Pauly: I'm home.
Ian: Good.

More dots got his hopes up, and then nothing. He didn't like that feeling, so he dove in.

Ian: Do you miss me yet?

Because he missed her. Being up here with his dad wasn't too far off from being alone. A lot of quiet. A lot of time for thinking. Especially when you weren't drinking.

Pauly: No. But I do miss the food.

She followed that up with a wagging tongue emoji.
He chuckled.

Ian: I knew you were a beans and potatoes and pork rind kinda girl.

She responded with a green, ill-looking emoji.

Ian: When I get back to Arlington, I'll make it up to you. I'll cook you a real meal, and then you can decide who's better. Me or Caceres.

More dots. This time, when they disappeared, they disappeared for a long time. Ian was lamenting having lost her when a new text appeared.

Pauly: I don't know. I'll have to think about it.

She was putting on the brakes now, but he couldn't get the sound of her breathy, "Okay," out of his head. She'd felt it, too. This heat between them. It might be wrong from a team standpoint, but at least is wasn't one-sided.

Ian: Fair enough. But just so we're clear, I only want to cook you a meal so I can get you into bed.
Pauly: Didn't work for Caceres.
Ian: Then he didn't do it right.

Those damn dots. He was going to be seeing them in his sleep.

Pauly: Good night, Pratt.
Ian: Good night, Byrne.

He couldn't wait to see her again.

Chapter Eight

Dressing in her private locker room two doors down from the rest of the team, Pauly kept an eye on the time. About thirty minutes before practice started, her phone rang. She snatched it off the top shelf of her locker. Her mother. Between Pauly's baseball schedule and her mother's full-time job at the bank plus extra hours spent cleaning professional buildings, they didn't get to talk much anymore. Texts were their primary form of communication, and texts just weren't the same.

"Hey, Mom!"

"How's my warrior princess?"

Pauly smiled. "Getting ready for practice. What's going on there?"

Tasha Byrne did this weird little sniff anytime she wanted to skirt a certain subject. It surprised Pauly she could hear the noise over the phone.

"The usual," Tasha said. "Are you ready for playoffs?"

And there was the detour. "I'm getting there. Looking forward to being back on the field." After a few days of distractions she didn't need.

"I got my time off approved so I'm gonna get to see you play."

"Awesome. And the boys? They're coming with you, right?"

There was a strange pause. "And your dad."

"But he was just here, and he said he couldn't take off again until maybe the championship series."

"P, he got laid off."

"Wait. What? He has seniority. They can't lay him off." Her throat tightened around the words.

"They did. They laid off the older guys and the newer guys. The guys in between got to stay. People just aren't watching cable like they used to, and nobody else is hiring installers, especially not installers your father's age."

Shit. "What about health benefits?"

"I got 'em through the bank."

Yeah, but her dad had been with the cable company for twenty-five years. It was the bread of their income.

Pauly felt flush. She reached behind her for the folding chair. "This sucks."

"I know, but I don't want you worrying about it. He has some feelers out. Your brothers have offered to chip in if things get tight. We'll manage."

No thanks to her. The apartment. The car. The insurance premiums. The extra cash infusions they sent when her back account got low.

"I'm getting old, and I'm tired," he'd said that day at Foley's when he'd told her about the Holymount coaching position. And she'd thought about it, off and on, since then, but she hadn't thought about it seriously enough to send in her resume.

Until now …

She wanted to be a ballplayer. She never wanted to be a burden.

When she jogged onto the field a few minutes later with her mitt tucked beneath her arm and a dark cloud over her head, she told herself sending in a resume wouldn't change anything in the foreseeable future. She still wanted a championship. She still planned to work like hell to get noticed by a scout. The sky brightened, and her steps grew lighter. Her mind refocused, and her senses turned sharp. She soaked in the sun and the warm-wind chaser, and she lapped the field, calm and completely in control. Things would work out.

"Byrne."

Crap. She took a stutter step and ran faster, hoping to leave him in her dust.

But he caught up to her with a grin, which brought back memories of their run along the river. The laughter. The connection. The inevitability.

Pauly, I'm going to kiss you.

"Pratt," she said gruffly, scattering the memories and veering off the warning track. She bent to pick up a stray ball rolling toward her and looked for its owner. Maybe she could slip into light tosses with someone else and leave Ian behind.

But nobody seemed to be missing a ball. And not even Flynn was interested in what she was doing with Pratt way out in center field.

"I got a question for you," Ian said. His voice was loud, and it carried on the wind.

"No," she said, much quieter than him. "Not here." Nothing personal on the field. Nothing that could throw off her game. "Quit yapping, and start throwing." She tossed the ball to him, and he barehanded it.

Then he retrieved his glove from the crook of his arm and backed up until he was squarely in the grass.

She backed up too, cherishing the space between them, knowing the gap would only get wider the longer they tossed.

Ian chucked the ball to her, and she chucked it back. Every time he opened his mouth, she shook her head to quiet him.

"I mean it, Pratt." She zipped her fingers over her closed lips. "Nothing that'll mess with my concentration."

He grinned, and that was bad enough.

Back and forth, the ball whizzed between them, landing in their gloves with satisfying thuds. Eventually, Ian faded in a blur of details. The sun. The air. The stretch and release of her arm. The loosening in her shoulder and elbow. The rhythm of it all lulled her into a peaceful oblivion.

Other guys moved closer, lining up to throw.

Ian shouted a jab at Sam Sutter and his shiny new cleats.

"I'm thick with the team owner," Sutter said. "She gave me these."

"Whaddya have to do to get 'em?" Caceres teased.

Pauly chuckled. Back and forth, she zeroed in on the ball.

"Byrne, how was camp?" Sanchez was in the mix now, too.

Pauly glanced at him sideways. "Campy," she said, feeling her pulse at the base of her throat.

"She caught a fish." Ian didn't look the least bit uncomfortable talking about their weekend. In fact, he looked proud.

"I caught multiple fish."

The other guys made varying noises that said they were impressed.

"Fishes?" Rodrigues asked.

"Just fish, dude," Caceres said. "Tell your ESL teacher to work on that."

"And unlike Carlyle, Byrne hooks the worm all by herself," Ian continued, and the other guys laughed.

Carlyle raised his mitt to catch a ball at the same time he flipped Ian off with his left hand. "While you were hooking worms, I was hooking up."

At that point, Pauly would've given anything for a subject change. The best she could do was focus on the baseballs whizzing by and popping into gloves all around her.

Thankfully, Coach Slater summoned them to the dugout after that, and she took off, jogging ahead of the pack.

Ian caught up to her in no time. "My dad refused to call anyone on your list," Ian said.

She glanced over her shoulder and, deciding there was enough space between them and everyone else, said, "That sucks."

"Yep. So I ended up calling them."

It was more than she expected, and she couldn't find her words.

"Aren't you going to ask me how it went?" He leaned forward to look at her face, which was partially obstructed by her ball cap.

"Not here," she said. "Nothing personal on the field. Remember?"

"Okay. Then how 'bout you come to my place tonight? I'll make you dinner." He wiggled his brows.

Asshole. She mentally scratched the hell out of that word. *Idiot.* "I'll pass."

"Then how 'bout we meet at Foley's … for a pitcher of root beer?" He grinned and shifted to a backpedal. "One of the attorneys agreed to give me fifteen free minutes of legal advice over the phone, and I'd like to be prepared. Since nobody prepares like you do, I thought …"

She *did* prepare like it was nobody's business.

"Fine," she said. "Five o'clock at Foley's." But then she actually heard what she was saying, and root beer or not, all things considered, it didn't seem right to meet at a bar. "Scratch that. Let's do Denny's."

He laughed. "Trade the brew for a banana split. Excellent idea. Always thinking, Byrne. I like that about you."

Always *overthinking.* Like now, when she couldn't stop wondering why she was kidding herself by agreeing to meet under the guise of helping him, when they both knew where more alone time would lead.

That right there was enough to prove she should cancel tonight.

But Denny's with Ian was better than sitting at home with a protein bar, trying to convince herself she could be happy in Holymount, New Jersey, next season.

• • •

Turned out, Denny's on a Thursday evening in Arlington was filled with enough old people to make Pauly think she'd taken a wrong turn and walked through the doors of a nursing home. But that comforted her, because a bunch of senior citizens weren't going to recognize or care about her and Ian Pratt. Which meant she could relax and enjoy his company.

As much as she wanted to turn off her feelings, she couldn't. So, she decided to feel them but not act on them. She would concentrate on their harmless commonalities and enjoy hanging out with someone who liked to talk baseball as much as she did. And in the process, they would win a championship.

It made perfect sense to her.

"All I know is the Royals are going to shoot themselves in the foot if they don't acquire Manly before August 31," she said.

Ian nodded while he sipped Coke through a straw. A lock of sandy hair fell in his eye, making him look a little bit like the boy in the pictures she'd found. But then he straightened, squared his broad shoulders, and turned the full weight of his sharp eyes and chiseled face in her direction.

There was nothing cute about that.

"Maybe they think they don't need him for the postseason," he said.

"That's crazy." *I'm crazy.*

"I think so, too. But I'm not a GM, and I wouldn't want to be. Too much pressure."

"But if you love the business of baseball, you would thrive under the pressure."

"I'll stick with landscaping," he said.

She wasn't surprised. And yet, he'd called all the attorneys when his father wouldn't, so clearly, there was a side of him that was willing to step up.

"There's a serious side of you, Pratt. You're taking care of this foreclosure thing."

"Only because I have to. Trust me. When it's resolved, I'm not going to be serious about anything for a very long time. Maybe never."

"What if you meet somebody?" She had no idea why she'd asked it.

"I don't do relationships. Getting serious is an absolute guarantee you're going to fuck it up. At least that's been my experience."

Okay. So he'd been burned. Or he'd burned somebody else. She didn't need to know the details. "Did your mom and dad get along?"

"Sometimes. When I was little mostly." He pushed a cherry through a clump of whipped cream at the bottom of his dish.

She looked from his mostly eaten dessert to his half-empty, third refill of Coke and wondered if he wished it was beer. Then she looked at her salad plate.

"I'm sorry you're facing this foreclosure alone," she said.

"I'm not alone." He flashed a smile. "I got you."

The way he said it, all sultry and confident. *I got you.* Her ovaries tingled.

Thankfully, her phone buzzed against the table.

She went from one uncomfortable situation to another when she recognized the Holymount, New Jersey, area code and exchange. *Cripes.* She'd just sent in that resume two hours ago. She thought she'd have more time than this to prepare.

"Take it," Ian said. "I'll just be over here lickin' the bowl."

"I don't want to," she said mindlessly, wishing she'd ordered a banana split.

"Why not?"

"I, uh …" Her gaze was still anchored on his ice cream.

"Here." He slid the bowl toward her. "Have some before you drool all over the place."

She gasped in defense. "I'm not drooling."

He grinned and pushed the bowl even closer. "I know you want it."

Okay, now she was drooling, and she was looking right at him. She dipped her spoon into the bowl and quartered off a piece of banana just to put the brakes on this crazy train. But when she put it into her mouth, he watched her with enough intensity to burn the place down. It was all she could do to swallow.

"Why didn't you want to answer that call?" He left his bowl in the middle of the table and filled his spoon again.

She didn't have to tell him anything, but she wanted to unload on someone. "I think it was someone from Holymount. About the coaching position. I sent in my resume."

He frowned. "Giving up on us already?"

They were loaded words. "I'm not giving up on anything. I just found out my dad's been laid off, and I have to think about a Plan B whether I like it or not."

Ian sucked a hefty ice cube into his mouth and crushed it with one snap of his jaw. As he chewed, he studied her. "But you don't like it. At all. If you did, you would've answered the call."

"That doesn't change anything."

"It should."

"Says the guy who plays baseball for the fun of it." She drew quote marks in the air around that last bit. "Lucky son of a bitch."

"You could play for the fun of it, too. If you made some adjustments."

She rolled her eyes. She wasn't about to ask him what adjustments he was referring to. "Try being the only woman in an entire baseball league, and then we'll talk."

"Ian?" The sweet voice invaded their conversation, causing them to turn in unison.

A short, curvy blonde in a frilly yellow dress approached the booth and smiled. She held hands with a miniature version of herself, and they stopped at the head of the table.

Ian smiled back. "Hi, Sara."

His tone was friendly, but Pauly noticed the bunched muscles in his neck and the way he picked the skin beside his thumbnail.

"Imagine running into you here," the woman said, glancing at Pauly and maintaining her warm expression.

"Not my normal night out," Ian said, still picking at his thumb.

"Mommy, who's that?" The little girl blushed when she looked at Ian, then she snuck a peek at Pauly before she buried her red cheeks in her mother's skirt.

"This is Ian, silly. Remember Mommy's friend? You've met him before. And this is …" Sara looked at Pauly expectantly.

"Pauly," Ian said. "*My* friend." He slipped Pauly a sultry look, and she swallowed a wave of heat. "Pauly, this is Sara …"

There should've been more after that, and Pauly was sure she wasn't the only one waiting for it. The atmosphere went from hot and loaded to awkward and clammy in the silence that followed.

"Nice to meet you, Sara," Pauly said, holding out her hand.

"It's really nice to meet you, too." Sara gave Pauly's hand a hearty shake and then looked at Ian. "I'm glad I ran into you. You look happier than I've seen you in a long time. Truly." She patted his back. "We won't keep you. Enjoy your dessert."

Weird.

When Sara and her daughter walked away, Pauly settled her attention on Ian. "What was that about?"

He stared into the space above her head, a blank expression on his face. "Honestly? I think she thinks you're my girlfriend."

"And you're okay with that?"

"It's better than her thinking I'm broken."

"So she's the one."

"What?"

"The one that either got burned or burned you."

A laugh caught in the back of Ian's throat, but he didn't look at her. "Nobody got burned. Neither one of us was happy. She said I was too much like my old man."

Pauly chewed on the inside of her lip. She'd gotten to know a different side of Ian, but she still wondered exactly how much of his father was in him.

There was a long, almost anguished pause before he asked, "Who are you like? Mom or Dad?"

"Probably my dad. But there's a little of both in me."

"Exactly. And your parents are pretty good people?"

She nodded.

"Lucky you." His smile was weak.

And, again, she thought about his mother and his reaction to that letter, and she couldn't shake the feeling that she was missing pieces. "Your mom was a good person, wasn't she?"

He reached for his Coke and drank until air rattled inside the straw. Then he set the glass on the table and looked right through her. "My mom was sick." He pointed to his head. "She, uh …" He reached for the glass again, removed the straw, jiggled the ice, and tipped the glass back against his mouth until he'd sucked out a few more drops. "She was honorably discharged for being diagnosed as bipolar."

"That's sad." From the letter, Pauly could tell the woman had believed in what she was doing overseas, and having her mission cut short must've been devastating.

"Yeah, well, that's not all." Ian looked pale now, and she wanted to reach across the table and grab his hand and tell him he didn't have to say another word, but he forged ahead. "She committed suicide."

Oh, God.

"As much as I loved my mom, I'm okay with being like my old man," he added.

"Ian …" Pauly hurt all over, but she knew it was nothing compared to the pain he felt. She looked at him deeply, making sure he knew she meant it when she said, "I'm so sorry your mom was sick, but we're more than the sum of our parents. A lot more."

"I'd like to think that."

"Then think it. Nobody's stopping you but you." She lifted her chin and gave him a confident look meant to snap him out of the self-pity.

And somehow, it worked.

His expression brightened. "Byrne, you're something else."

"What does that even mean?"

"I don't know." His lips twitched, and he stared at her long and hard. "Just know it's a good something else."

The kind of good something that made her heart warm.

Chapter Nine

Ian walked alongside Pauly in the Denny's parking lot. Her strides were short and jerky. Her hair bounced against her shoulders and back. She was talkative, but something seemed … off. They'd passed Sara's table on their way out, and he wondered if that had anything to do with it.

"Do you know the guy she's with?" Pauly asked.

"Steve? Yep. He's her husband. We went to high school together. Different classes. He's older." Ian flashed Pauly a look. "Couldn't you tell?"

"Oh, definitely. He looks ancient."

"Good answer."

"You're *way* better looking."

She'd definitely stressed the "way."

"I am?" He angled his body toward her and gave her a look that said he was pleased and she could keep going.

She closed her eyes and shook her head, a faint smile on her lips. "Just keeping it real."

Right there. Something odd again.

"How long have they been married?" she asked.

"Don't know. By the looks of the kids, I'd say two or three years."

"And how long ago did you break up?"

"Jesus, Byrne. Why are you obsessing?"

"I don't know. I … There's just something about them. I'm curious."

"Gathering data?" He scratched at a random itch on his neck. "But there's no problem to solve here."

"I know."

They walked a little farther in silence. He'd parked at the front of the lot, but she'd parked in the back. Couldn't risk a scratch on her lily-white Nissan. So, he'd decided to be a gentleman and walk her to her car.

"I never think much about having kids, but seeing that makes me wonder if I'll make a good mom," she said. "You know, someday, after baseball."

"I vote yes."

Actually, he voted for talking about something other than Sara's happy family, because he was decently wigged out by seeing her, too.

"Maybe that's another plus for Holymount," Pauly said, and he hated that she was trying to talk herself into this. "I can finally start something I can finish." She frowned. "Baseball has destroyed my love life. Flynn and Craig want to fix me up, but I'm worried whoever they find will be intimidated by me."

"You're very intimidating." He was only partly sarcastic.

"I know. It sucks." She genuinely looked crushed by the thought of it.

"Okay." He stopped walking. "You actually met my ex-girlfriend. The least you can do is tell me about your last boyfriend." Because he had a feeling some of her reaction was rooted in that.

"Tyler," she said, slowing to a stop too. "His name is Tyler." Tension radiated off her.

"And what does Tyler do?" Since she'd said she wasn't into athletes …

"He's a DJ. Almost famous." She looked away, toward the horizon. "He didn't like baseball."

Ian laughed. "Then why was he dating a baseball player?"

"He said he put up with that part because he thought it was temporary."

"Dude didn't know you very well."

She looked at him again, and a faint smile brightened her face. "Of course, he didn't tell me those things until he was breaking up with me, so I wasted two years thinking I was in love with someone who loved me too. All of me." The frown came back. "I won't make that mistake again."

For some reason, he thought that was a crying shame. Sunlight flickered in her shiny black hair, and despite the obvious sadness, a fire glowed behind her silver eyes. Tyler was a fucking idiot, because Pauly was downright magical, and Ian wanted to show her just how much he appreciated all of her right here. But he doubted she would take him up on his offer.

"So, Flynn's going to find me somebody. A *lawyer*. And I'm going to have some fun. Ease back into the dating scene. Blow off some steam. And not worry about love or relationships until my playing days are over."

Well, if that was what she wanted …

Ian shifted closer and pinned her with his gaze. "You know, it's not nice to talk about other men when you're on a date with someone else."

She coughed a laugh. "We aren't dating."

"Call it whatever you want, but this is a date. Two people. Talking. Sharing ice cream. Flirting. It's got date written all over it."

"I can't date you. You're my teammate."

"You can't kiss me either, but you agreed to that. I don't see what the big deal is. I like you. You like me. Neither one of us is looking for anything serious, relationship-wise." He smiled. "We're both committed to winning a championship. Where's the problem with two consenting adults enjoying each other's company privately?"

She scoffed but eyed him up. "It's a bad idea."

"Holding back is a bad idea. It just clogs your head with more shit to worry about. My way, you get to have fun *and* a clear head. I say, for once, we do it my way."

She tackled him. Pressed her body against his, sending him backward a few steps. It was just like Pauly Byrne to attack a batter head-on. Ian's lips quirked with rising laughter as her mouth covered his, and then, suddenly, nothing felt funny anymore.

Her arms snaked around his back. Her fingers dug into his spine. It was hot and hurried. A gnash of teeth. A tangle of tongues. An explosion of flavors. Bananas, strawberries, whipped cream, and something else, something uniquely Pauly. He shoved a hand into the hair at the base of her neck and tilted her head back, opening her mouth wider. He splayed his other hand across her tight ass.

She moaned, and he went hard.

They'd gone from zero to 210 in two seconds. Any more, and he'd be coaxing her into the backseat of her car.

And he would've done it, too, if he thought for a minute she wouldn't have regrets about moving so fast—in public.

Ian dragged his mouth away from hers and set his hands in a neutral position on her hips. "Pauly," he said huskily.

She tipped her head back, looking as dazed as he felt. "I took it too far. I'm sorry."

"I'm not," he said. Her body was still pressed against his— warm and pliant—and he didn't try to move her.

"I want to try it your way, but I don't want things to be weird between us."

"Doesn't feel weird to me." Unless he counted the erection being strangled by his jeans.

"Good. Because baseball is the most important thing in the world to me."

"I know that."

She closed her eyes briefly and then stepped back. "Can we dial it back?"

He chuckled. "You were the one who jumped me. Again, not that I'm complaining."

She held his gaze as she nodded. "This goes against everything I've been taught."

"What have you been taught?"

"Not to let anything with a penis make a fool out of me." She smiled, and he laughed. "So, if we proceed, we proceed with caution. No labels. No PDA."

"You just kissed me in a parking lot."

She shrugged. "Denny's doesn't count. The field, on the other hand …" She exhaled. "It's all business there. And if this affects the game in anyway, we're done. We go back to being teammates."

"Just like that?"

"Just like that."

"Okay. Ground rules laid." He bobbed his brows and thought about luring her into the backseat again, but the parking lot traffic was picking up. Cars pulled in and backed out. Pauly noticed it, too.

Her eyes flicked back and forth between people moving to and from their vehicles, until she finally said, "Maybe we should call it a night."

Knowing her level of determination, it wasn't an argument he could win, so he nodded. "Night, Pauly."

"Night, Ian."

He watched her get into her car and close the door. He watched her pull away. He'd never been one to obsess about a woman or a game, but he hoped like hell they won on Saturday.

He didn't want to give her any reason not to tackle him like that again.

• • •

Keeping that kiss off her mind took super-human focus, but Pauly managed. She managed at morning practice. She managed on the four-hour bus ride to Charleston, West Virginia. And she managed—mostly—while she was in the visiting clubhouse for Coach Slater's pregame speech. Now, she just had to manage for a minimum of six innings, while she was staring right at Ian.

You got this. Her mind was a steel-tight vault, powered by details and fortified by focus.

Ian and a few other teammates passed her in the hallway as she made her way to the ladies' room. She nodded. Played it cool.

Sutter tipped his cap. "How you feeling, Ace?"

"Good. Ready."

"Excellent."

They all kept moving in their respective directions, but not before someone swatted her ass.

Pauly's cheeks heated. She didn't dare look back to see if the culprit was Ian. Maybe it wasn't. And even if it was, so what? Ass taps of encouragement were common in baseball. They didn't count as PDA.

Chill. Focus on the Now. And yes, she thought of it with a capital "n" because it was the key to pitching a good game. Ninety minutes until the first pitch. She needed to pee—two floors up—and then she could shut herself in the broom closet where the Charleston Miners had stashed her to give her privacy while she dressed. She hated away games and the substandard accommodations.

"Byrne."

She stopped before reaching the double doors to the stairs. Coach Slater traveled the hallway behind her.

"Yes, sir?"

He wiggled two fingers, motioning for her to come closer. Something about the set of his jaw made her think she was in trouble. *Big trouble.*

She filled with a sense of dread.

"You going to be able to focus out there?" His voice was stern.

"Absolutely."

"You would tell me if you're having any doubts?"

"Always."

"Good. I would hate to see you sell yourself short and check out of this season before it's over."

"Nobody's checking out, sir." Least of all her. "I'm in this to win this."

"Good to hear. We can talk about Holymount *after* we hoist the trophy."

Now, he was making sense. "You know about Holymount? How? I haven't even interviewed yet."

"When a university is considering hiring a woman to coach NCAA baseball, it's big news in my circles, so keep your head on straight. I have a feeling it's only going to get crazier." He swatted her ass with a clipboard as he walked away.

She exhaled. *Damn it.* She didn't need things to get crazier. It was time to dig deep, block out the noise, and throw laser beams. Easy enough.

But two hours later, with the score tied at zero, nothing seemed easy. Pauly had walked the bases loaded. Her mind was a vault, all right. She couldn't extract a single usable piece of information on the batters she faced.

Ian freed his head from his helmet and his face from his cage. He took the long walk to the mound extra slow, and she shook him off the whole way. *He* was the last thing she needed.

"Don't be such a hard-ass," he said. "Let me help you. You need a redirect, and I can give it."

"I don't need you to rescue me, Pratt. I need you to leave me alone. And if you smack my ass again, I'm going to break your fingers."

"What? I didn't touch you. *Today.*" He flashed a smile and then hid it behind the webbing of his glove. "What do you know about this guy?"

"Nothing. My mind is blank. Abso-fucking-lutely blank. That's why there are men on."

The home-plate ump took a step toward them.

"Then here's what we're going to do. We're going to role-play. You be Randy Johnson, and I'll be Robby Hammock. Turner Field, baby. Perfect game. You read me?" He started to back away. "Take my head off. I dare ya." He grinned and jogged away.

This wasn't going to work. She didn't role-play like an elementary schooler. She made calculated decisions. She threw deliberate pitches. And *that* worked … when she knew what to throw.

Ian pulled his mask over his face and squatted behind the plate. He tapped one finger on his left thigh.

Fastball.

She couldn't remember shit about this batter. A fastball could be suicide. She almost shook off Ian's pitch call, but he pointed at her, and she took it as a challenge. He wanted her to take his head off. Fine. He needed some sense knocked into him for thinking they could effortlessly navigate a no-strings personal relationship while they were in the middle of the playoffs. She did, too. But she was the one with the ball.

And she kept the ball, from that point on, through seven miraculously scoreless innings.

"You had me worried for a minute," Coach Slater said when he told her she wasn't going back out for the eighth.

"I feel great," she said, breathless. "Better than ever."

"You look good, too, but I'm not going to ruin you on Game One. Take a seat. Rest that arm. Be proud of the game you threw."

Ian leaned forward from his spot on the bench, his elbows and strong forearms balanced on his thighs. He grinned, winked, and then sat back.

He may not have smacked her ass in the hallway, but he'd saved her ass on the field. And God help her, with adrenaline and endorphins coursing through her veins, making her muscles twitchy, she *really* wanted to thank him with another kiss. But she couldn't. She wouldn't. Not in Charleston. Not on the team's time. This series was best of five. Assuming they ended on the right side of the scoreboard tonight, they would need two more wins—one tomorrow night in Charleston and one a few days from now in Arlington—to claim the divisional title. Then, they would move on to the championship series. Pauly could taste it.

She could taste something else, too.

The good news was, after pitching seven scoreless innings, it was clear kissing Ian hadn't messed with her game. In fact, it might have improved it. When she looked at it like that, it only made sense to kiss him again as soon as they were back in Arlington.

Chapter Ten

"Listen up!" Coach Slater stood at the front of the bus in the middle of the aisle, gripping seat backs in both hands, when they pulled into the Federal Field parking lot a little after 9:00 p.m. on Sunday evening. Charleston had been a forty-eight-hour whirlwind, with Coach keeping everyone on a short leash. Early to bed. Early to rise. On the field at all points in between. But it had paid off with back-to-back wins, and Ian was happy to be back home in Arlington.

Guys who weren't sleeping piped down, and guys who'd managed to doze off during the three-hour drive perked up. Ian had been way too wired to fall asleep.

"Go home. Go to bed early. I'll see you back here at noon for BP. Game Three tomorrow, people." Then he pointed to the back of the bus where the usual suspects, including Ian, were sitting. "I'll be calling Foley's to make sure none of your asses are parked at that bar. You hear me?"

Carlyle groaned. Sanchez hollered up a, "Yes, sir, Skip." Rodrigues parroted the sentiment, and Ian simply smiled. Because, for once, beer was the last thing on his mind.

The top of Pauly's head reached above a seat back in the second row, where she sat next to Louie Flynn, among the pitchers. Sometime during the trip, she'd piled her curly hair on top of her head, and all Ian could think of now was shoving his fingers into the beautiful mess and letting it all come tumbling down. But after Coach's warning, he knew the odds of anything close to that happening were slim to none. Hell, she still refused to talk to him candidly in front of everyone else. But a man could dream, and he didn't mind the idea of going home to bed if it meant dreaming about her.

By the time Ian grabbed his gear and shook off the guys, who were determined to eke out some sort of trouble Coach Slater wouldn't hear about, he'd completely given up on seeing Pauly tonight—unless he did something ballsy, like text her.

He considered that as he walked to his truck, which sat in the shadows at the back of the emptying lot. He hadn't parked back there because he cared about his truck but because he'd arrived a little late on Friday, after his meeting with a foreclosure attorney had run long. He'd been semi-pissed about that on Friday, but the next time he saw that attorney, Ian was going to have to thank him, because tonight, only one other car remained in his row. A white Nissan.

Ian smiled.

Pauly rolled down her window as he approached. "You're slow," she teased.

"I didn't know anyone was waiting for me."

Even in the dark, he could see the sparkle in her eyes. "Just wanted the chance to say more than two words to you." She grinned. "Thank you."

"That's two words," he said, chuckling.

"Then how 'bout 'thank you for what you did for me on the mound'?"

"You thanked me in Charleston."

"Yeah, but I'm not sure I thanked you *properly*." Her brows rose.

"Tell me what you have in mind, and I'm sure we can work something out."

She looked out her windshield at the empty parking lot. Ian looked too, in time to see the bus pull away. She opened her door and stood before him, eyes wide and shining in the moonlight.

They'd been in a similar position before, in the Denny's parking lot, and the memory raised his pulse.

"What are you up to, Byrne?"

She glanced at the bags crisscrossing his body. "Lose the gear."

"Done." He crossed two empty parking spots and tossed the bags into the bed of his truck.

When he turned around, she was there, moving into him until he grabbed her around the waist and pinned her against the tailgate.

"Do you think anyone will see us back here?" She balanced on the bumper and wrapped her legs around his hips, tugging a groan from his throat.

"I don't care." He traced her jaw with his thumb. "And after the way you pitched in Charleston, you shouldn't either. What are they going to do? Bench us?" He scoffed. "When you're good, you can get away with anything."

She flashed a saucy smile and pulled him closer with her legs, palming his chest, cranking up the pleasure until he was good and hard. "Thank you," she whispered a second before she fisted his sweatshirt and pulled him into a hot kiss.

He leaned into her, pressing his weight against the warmth between her legs, using the truck as leverage. His body was practically vibrating from wanting her. He swept his tongue over hers, sucked her bottom lip into his mouth, and slipped a hand beneath her shirt, where his fingertips road the waves of her rib cage. After that, nothing registered. He lost himself. In the way she tasted. In the way she felt. In the things she did deep inside of him.

She squeezed his hips between her thighs, arched her heat against his erection, and his breath released on a low growl. He wanted her sprawled out and naked in the bed of the truck. And he wanted it bad. Bad enough to cup her fine ass and lift her up.

She whimpered and tossed her head back, giving him access to her throat. He took it greedily, sucking and licking and dragging his teeth and open mouth over every inch of skin.

"I told you I was thankful," she said, her throaty laughter breaking the quiet.

"*Very* thankful."

She shuddered at his breathy words in her ear, and he lifted his head to look at her. Eyes glazed over. Lips full. He'd never seen anything so fucking hot.

"That kiss in the Denny's parking lot," she said, breathless, running her hands over his back until they tucked possessively into the waistband of his jeans.

"Was nothing compared to this one." He pressed her against the truck again and nuzzled her neck.

"True, but … it brought me good luck." She sucked in a breath when he thumbed her hardened nipple through her bra.

He lifted his head. "You think the kiss is why you pitched a good game?"

"It definitely didn't hurt."

He laughed loudly. "So are you kissing me now because you want *me* or because you want to keep pitching lights out?"

"I want it all," she said, grinning as she nipped at his lips. "I'm greedy that way."

Desire rumbled in his throat. "Then I'm going to give it to you."

Ian covered her mouth with his and prepared to make good on his words, but a vibration in his back pocket distracted him.

"What?" she asked against his lips, dragging her mouth to his cheek.

"Nothing. Just my phone. Who the hell would be calling this late?"

She pulled back. "See who it is."

Something didn't feel right, but he shook his head. "Probably those idiots wanting to get into trouble."

She nodded, traced a finger along the line of his jaw and down the side of his neck, and still, something didn't feel right. "Check it," she said. "Just in case."

He slipped the phone from his back pocket and saw the missed caller had been his dad, and something felt dead wrong now. "He never calls me," Ian said, dialing him back.

Pauly unlocked her legs from around his hips and slipped out from between him and the tailgate. "I hope everything's okay."

"Maybe it was just a butt dial." But nobody answered. Ian ended the call and tried again.

"Go check on him." Concern flashed in her eyes, and something warmed in his chest. "Go." With a squeeze of his hand, she stepped back, moving closer to her car. "I should be listening to Coach anyway. Home to bed."

He wanted to join her so badly it hurt, but for the first time in forever, a strong sense of duty won out over the opportunity for fun. "I'll call you later."

"But not too late." She smiled softly. "Game tomorrow."

When they were both in their respective vehicles, Ian followed her Nissan out of the parking lot, placing a never-ending chain of calls to his father, hoping it was all just an inconvenient mistake. He reached the house on the outskirts of town in record time and noticed the lights were on in the living room. No one answered when Ian knocked, which wasn't unusual, considering how loud his father kept the television. Except, when Ian walked in, the place was dead quiet.

"Dad?"

From the entryway, Ian wandered into the cluttered kitchen. Stacks of dirty dishes glowed in the yellow, under-cabinet lighting. Open containers of food littered the counters. Something sticky tugged on the bottom of his shoe. *Jesus*, it smelled like something had died in here.

He raised his T-shirt over his nose. "Dad!"

From the kitchen, Ian passed into the family room, finally finding his father passed out in the reclining chair. For one heart-stopping second, he worried Ray might be dead. But, the motor, as he called his father's snoring, started up as soon as Ian got closer.

White whiskers lined Ray's jaw and upper lip. Deep, dark circles lived beneath his eyes. His thin skin sagged and wrinkled, making him look much older than fifty-five. And on the end table sat an almost empty bottle of vodka atop his father's phone.

Ian closed his eyes for a second to get his bearings. When he opened them, he saw a few sheets of paper in Ray's lap. Although it wasn't technically Ian's business, he gathered up the pages and read them.

More bad news. This house and the detached mechanic's garage had fallen into foreclosure, too.

Ian went numb, and then he turned angry. All these years, he'd given his dad the benefit of the doubt, thinking the booze was just a coping mechanism. But this wasn't coping. And this couldn't be fixed by Ian meeting with attorneys and winning ten grand. Pauly was right. Ray needed rehab.

Ian hoped she was right about something else, too. That they were more than the sum of their parents. Because if she was wrong about that, Ian was doomed.

"Dad!" Ian kicked his father's boot and jostled his shoulder. "Wake up. We need to talk." His heart was racing. "Dad!"

The man snorted and stirred. "Fuckin' wake the dead, boy."

"That's the idea," Ian snapped. "You been drinking?"

"A little."

"A lot." Ian snatched the bottle of vodka from the end table and went to the kitchen for some water.

"Hey!" Ray called in protest.

"You're not gonna need this where you're going."

"I ain't going nowhere."

With water in hand, Ian stalked back to his father. "The way I see it, you've got two choices. One, you stay here, you keep drinking, and you die in this chair, or two, you check into the hospital for detox."

"Hell no," his father slurred.

"Then I'm done," Ian said, throwing up his hands, wishing he'd never cut short his night with Pauly for this. "If you won't help yourself, I'm not going to help you anymore either. You can rot for all I care." He didn't mean a word of it, but the hurtful words tumbled out and piled up between them like an impenetrable wall.

"Get the fuck out," Ray said. "Go on."

But Ian couldn't move. He didn't know what to do. He didn't know how to get a grown man to do something he didn't want to do. He didn't know how to prove to the man that life could get better—if he let it get better. Ian's words reverberated in his head: *Then I'm done.* Because things got too heavy. That's where his mom had been. That's exactly where his dad was now, too. *Done.* Ian couldn't shake the gut-clenching fear that if he left, Ray would never get up.

"Dad, look at me." Desperation filled Ian's voice as he knelt beside the chair and gripped his father by the shoulders. "I didn't mean that. I'm not done. I'm just frustrated. We can do this the easy way, or we can do this the hard way. Either way, I'm not leaving here until I get through to you, because you're not done either."

Ray swung at him, but the man was far too drunk to meet his mark. Ian caught his feeble hand mid-swing. For maybe the first time in his life, he held his father's hand, and he held on tight.

"Do you really want me to bury both my parents before I'm thirty?" Ian asked. "Do you really want me to lose more than I already have?" The fact that his voice shook wasn't lost on him. "Do *you* really want to lose more than you already have?"

The heavy shit just got heavier, and Ian questioned every decision he'd made since he'd left the stadium lot. But then Ray closed his eyes and slumped sideways in the chair, and to Ian's horror, the man sobbed.

It was a god-awful, slaughterhouse wail that went on for what seemed like hours. Every time Ian tried to talk, Ray sobbed louder. So, with no other means of comforting the man, Ian simply held his hand until the crying stopped.

Finally, Ian said, "You can do this, Dad. You can get better, but you need help. Wasn't that what you always told Mom? Don't you wish she would've listened?"

Ray nodded. He slurred something about Barbie never listening, and then he reached for Ian, giving him a sloppy, heartbroken hug.

Ian wallowed in the sorrow and magnitude of what was facing them for only a minute. Then, he lifted Ray from the chair in a stronger, hopeful hug and led the man to the door.

••••

A little after midnight, Pauly looked through the peephole on her front door and wasn't one bit surprised to see Ian. She was more surprised it had taken him so long to get here.

She opened the door with a smile, assuming the fact that he was here meant his father was okay. "I thought you were going to call."

"I needed to see you." He looked a bit disheveled, but sexy, like maybe he'd driven around for the last couple hours trying to keep himself from coming here to ravish her. *Damn.* She wanted to be ravished, but not now. That phone call had been a blessing in disguise. They were a day away from wrapping up the divisional series. If they slept together tonight, everything would change, and she needed *every damn thing* to stay the same.

"Nothing else is going to happen, Ian. I'm serious. For now, we just kiss."

"In parking lots."

She smirked. "Exactly."

"Until the season is over."

"Maybe."

"Maybe not." There was something dangerous in his eyes. Unhinged.

She tightened her grip on the door. "Ian, it's late."

"I know. I … didn't want to go home." He sighed, and she saw the raw emotion for what it was—pure exhaustion. "I admitted my dad for detox."

"Oh my God." She caught his hand by the wrist. "Get in here. Why didn't you say so in the first place?"

"I couldn't find the words. And then I hoped maybe I wouldn't need any." Somehow, his tired eyes still managed to level a sultry invitation.

She did her best to ignore it, but it was hard to ignore over six feet of virile male when it stood in the middle of a studio apartment, sucking up 400 square feet of air.

"Sit," she said, brushing past him to the sofa, where she pushed aside throw pillows and patted the empty spot. "Tell me what happened."

He moved slowly and hovered above the cushion, looking pained and maybe even afraid. She slid her hand over his back as he sat.

"I found him passed out in his chair. The damn vodka bottle was on top his phone, so somehow it must've initiated the call." Ian leaned forward, elbows to knees. "I also found some papers that said his house and the garage are in foreclosure now, too."

"No." She rested her hand on his shoulder.

He nodded. "The guy's a fucking mess."

"How did you get him to go to the hospital?"

"It was brutal. He yelled at me. He tried to hit me. And that was the easy part." Ian exhaled noisily. "But I kept at him, and eventually he broke down." Emotion riddled his face. "That was the hardest part."

"I'm so sorry," she said again.

Ian reached across his body and laid a hand on hers. "It's my turn to thank you."

"For what?"

"You said he needed rehab. You left me that number. And you have this"—he squeezed her hand—"slightly annoying belief that I'm capable of doing better and being better, so I went with it. Thank you." He patted her hand and let it go.

She had the urge to wrap an arm around him and lay her head against his shoulder. Instead, she pushed simple words past the lump in her throat. "You're welcome."

Silence enveloped the room. She watched him, leaning forward, his shoulders rising and falling on each breath. They were definitely even now. And they were better together than they had been apart. Too bad it had taken her almost four full seasons to figure that out. Not that she would've pursued a serious relationship with a teammate. Not that she was doing that now.

"I should go," he said, rising off the couch an inch.

"Don't." She pressed her hand to his thigh, and he sat again. When their eyes met, she saw relief. "I was watching *Fast & Furious* for about the millionth time. You wanna watch with me?"

He leaned back, pressed deep into the sofa, and exhaled. "That sounds really good."

After that, he didn't say much, and his silence was strangely soothing. Having him there anchored her somehow. His presence made the silly movie meaningful instead of white noise to keep her from worrying too much about the next game. He made the room less empty and the couch more comfortable—even though they were sitting on opposite sides. And when he laughed, she laughed, too, mostly because for once, she wasn't lonely.

About halfway through the movie, he unzipped his sweatshirt, shrugged it off, balled it up behind his head, and said, "Don't let me overstay my welcome." And after flashing a smile, he drifted off to sleep.

This time, when Pauly got the urge to lean on him, she did. She crawled across the sofa and settled against his solid side, her legs tucked beneath her, her head on his broad chest. He stirred once to stretch his arm behind her neck and rest his hand on her shoulder. It was nice. Warm and easy. She closed her eyes and listened to his breathing, savoring the fresh scent of his laundry soap mixed with the woodsy scent of his cologne. She was falling for him, and that was stupid.

But when Pauly fell asleep, she dreamed they could stay like this forever.

Chapter Eleven

There was no such thing as being quiet in a studio apartment. Between the flushing toilet, running water, and the racket Ian was now making in the kitchen, it was only a matter of time before Pauly woke up.

She sat in her bed across the room from where he was cracking eggs against the rim of a stainless-steel bowl. Sleepy eyes. Silky scarf wrapped around her head. And a pouty mouth that made him want to forget about making omelets so he could make love to her instead. But they had a game today, and he didn't want to be labeled a distraction.

No labels. And he'd agreed. But after last night, something had changed. She could call him—or not call him—whatever she liked. But to him, she was a rock. His rock.

He waggled the spatula in her direction and smiled. "Morning, beautiful. Thanks for letting me sleep on your couch."

She nodded, covered her mouth when she yawned, and climbed out of bed. Without a word, she disappeared behind the headboard that shielded a tiny bathroom from the rest of the apartment.

He hummed while he whisked the eggs, tossing in some shredded cheese he'd found in the meat drawer. Him being here, cooking for her, might wig her out, but he would take his chances. With any luck, by the time he left, she would see what he saw. They were good together. On and off the field.

Pauly returned a few minutes later with her curls wrestled into a ponytail and a brighter expression on her face. She was still in the T-shirt from the night before, but instead of jeans, flannel boxers covered her bottom half. Casual. Cute. And damn sexy.

"What are you making?" she asked.

"Cheese omelets. I was limited by the lack of supplies. No recipes call for whey protein and recovery drinks."

She laughed. "I don't cook."

"I can see that."

"How'd you sleep?"

"Good. But you could've kicked me out, you know. I wasn't expecting to spend the night. I hope I didn't bother you. I don't snore or anything, do I?"

"No." She smiled sheepishly. "You're the perfect sleeper."

He grinned. It was an oddly pleasing compliment.

"I'm glad you could sleep after the night you had," she said. "I wasn't going to be mean and wake you up."

Far from it—she'd covered him with a quilt before she'd gone off to her own bed. He hadn't been "out" enough not to notice that.

"And that's why I'm cooking you breakfast." He nodded to the two-seater breakfast bar. "Sit, and let a man feed you."

She sat, but her eyes widened. "You know it wasn't too long ago when you told me you only wanted to cook for me so you could get me into bed."

There was something sultry in her voice, something that made her delivery sound like a come-on. If she was anyone but Pauly, he would've thought she knew exactly what she was doing. But they had to be at the field in less than four hours. He couldn't imagine she'd meant it to come out that way.

"You just got out of bed," he said with a smile. "Why would I want to send you back?"

"Good point." The corner of her mouth hitched, and she watched him work in silence. Every so often, he looked up at her, and when their eyes met, a jolt of something strong and intoxicating nearly put him on his ass.

"If you keep looking at me like that, I'm going to burn the eggs."

She laughed. "I don't know what you're talking about."

But she did. He could tell by the way she pulled her bottom lip between her teeth and struggled not to look at him again. And his blood hummed in his veins. He couldn't remember anything ever feeling so right.

"Are you going to see your dad before you go to the field?" she asked.

At the mention of his father, his body cooled. "No visitation. He can't have any contact with the outside world, but I can call for updates on his condition once a day."

"Wow. How long do they think he'll be in there?"

"Four or five days. I'm supposed to talk to a social worker about options for when he's discharged. They'll start him on a twelve-step program, and he'll need to keep up with that when he's out. I'm going to call his sister and see if she can come help. She helped after my mom died. I hope he doesn't need much more than that, because inpatient rehab costs a shitload."

"Damn," Pauly said softly. "I wish I could help."

"You already have." He slid a plated omelet toward her, and when she reached for her fork, he grabbed her hand and brought her knuckles to his lips for a quick kiss.

That smile was all he needed to get through this. She splayed her palm across his cheek and ran her thumb over his bottom lip, sending heat to his groin.

He pulled her hand away from his face and set it on the counter with a friendly pat. "If something crazy happens and you have to pitch tonight, what's your plan?"

"My plan?"

"Don't tell me you don't have a plan. You're Pauly Freaking Byrne." He set his plate on the counter in front of him and dug in. "When you take the mound, you always have a plan."

"Not this time," she said around a mouthful of egg. "I'm going to wing it. If something happens and Skip gives me the nod, I'm going to walk out there and pretend I'm Big Unit. It worked in Charleston." Even as she said it, she worried her bottom lip, and that worried him.

"I'm all for winging it," he said. "But it's nice to have a safety net. We should go over the reports. Better to be safe than sorry, you know?"

She gaped. "Who are you? Convincing your dad to get clean, keeping your hands to yourself even though I know it's killing you, cooking like you're Guy Fieri, and willingly going over scouting reports? I mean, seriously. Who *are* you?" She laughed, and he joined in.

Ian wasn't sure yet, but he was starting to really like this guy.

• • •

Coach Slater called on Pauly in the second inning, after John Boardman was pulled early. She pitched lights out, basically hand-delivering the divisional title to the Aces. Six innings had felt like a warmup, and she could've easily gone all nine. But Coach wanted her fresh for the championship series, which opened in Urbana, Illinois, on Sunday.

Due to Pauly's superstitious streak, Ian slept on her couch again the Friday night before they left, and the next morning, she kissed him soundly in the parking lot of her apartment complex. For good luck.

On Saturday, she spent most of the bus ride to Illinois breathing in through her nose and out through her mouth, visualizing perfect pitches. Every so often, Flynn flashed his phone screen at her.

"How about this one?" he'd say, offering up another covert picture of one of Craig's coworkers. "Beefcake?"

Pauly always answered the same. "Not now."

"Grab an itinerary as you exit," Coach Slater said from his usual spot at the front of the bus. He didn't have to yell over anyone, because the group had been eerily silent since the last rest stop. "When we aren't together as a team, we're in our rooms, reflecting on the job at hand. There's a championship on the other side of Urbana, people. Don't lose sight of that. See Marshall for room assignments and keys." He pointed to Quincy Marshall, who pulled double duty as the equipment manager and travel secretary. "I'll see everyone in the banquet room for dinner."

On the other side of the aisle from Pauly, fellow starting pitcher Matt Fry stuck a picture of his wife and kids into the fore edge of his bible and slipped the book into the backpack at his feet. "Here we go," he said, exhaling and making the sign of the cross.

Pauly admired his dedication, and even though she hadn't been inside a church in ages, she blessed herself, too.

They filed off the bus in near silence. Twenty-seven ballplayers, anxious as hell. She didn't look for Ian, except discreetly and to keep her distance. There was no room in her brain for anything but baseball now.

Once she was in her room, she called her father.

"How ya holdin' up?" he asked.

"Good. Focused. Ready to go. Where are you guys?"

"Stuck in traffic outside Columbus. We'll be stopping for the night soon and leaving bright and early in the morning."

"That's a lot of driving, Dad." Not to mention a lot of money in gas and hotel rooms. "Be careful."

"Of course. I gotta live to make it back to Arlington to see you pitch Game Four."

"We're going to wrap this up in three," she said, knowing the shortest distance between her and a championship was winning two games in Urbana and one in Arlington.

"Aim for four."

"I'm not going to root against my team."

"P, all I'm sayin' is if you pitch the winning game, it'll raise your stock. Can you imagine the hype surrounding you winning this with a strong Game-Four performance?"

That kind of hype could get her noticed. But …

"When you talk about raising my stock, you're talking about lowering someone else's." Like Boardman, who was still reeling from being pulled on Thursday. Or Fry, who was scheduled to pitch Game Two. "I don't want somebody to go out there and blow a game, just so I can get on the mound again this series."

But if that didn't happen, and she ended up going through with this interview and getting the coaching position at Holymount, tomorrow afternoon's start would be her last start. Ever.

Her stomach lurched.

"Thick skin wins the war, P."

"I know, Dad. I know." She pushed off the bed, feeling uncomfortable in her skin. "Text me when you guys stop for the night. I need to get downstairs for dinner."

She couldn't believe a five-minute phone call could ruin six hours of relative calm. Now, when she visualized pitches, in the back of her mind, she worried about never throwing one again. Three feet from her hotel room, a debilitating panic set in.

"Byrne, baby, Byrne." Hank Carlyle and Giovanni Caceres walked toward her, Fry and Sanchez behind them.

She liked Caceres, and she usually tolerated Carlyle, but tonight, she couldn't even smile as she joined them in the elevator.

Before the doors slid shut, someone called, "Hold it." And then a hand stuck through the gap.

With a clang and a jerk, the doors reopened, and Sam Sutter walked on with Ian.

Seven people fit on an elevator, but seven professional athletes had to jockey for space. Pauly ended up with a smiling Ian pressed against her left side.

She didn't acknowledge him. The pressure in her head started to rise.

While Carlyle's booming voice echoed off the stainless-steel walls, telling everyone about his latest run-in with the team's massage therapist, Ian lowered his voice and asked, "Everything okay?"

She didn't look at him, but she felt his warm, peppermint-scented breath on her cheek, and she wound even tighter. "Yep."

"Just focusing?"

Carlyle cackled. "She has massive tits. I swear. Ya'll should make appointments with her."

Every word grated on Pauly's already thin nerves.

"She bent over to rub my back, and I could feel them right here," he continued. "Nipples hard as rocks."

Pauly winced. She tried to relieve some of the pressure with an exhale.

"Christ, Carlyle," Ian said, looking uncomfortable, too.

"What? She wanted me. I could tell. I was shirtless. Who wouldn't?" The idiot literally flexed in the elevator, and Pauly ground her back teeth together. "So I told her I had something special she could rub, and I took her hand and—"

It was foul, and it was the final straw. Pauly cracked. She pushed off Ian and poked a finger into Carlyle's bicep. "That's sexual harassment, you fucking idiot."

"Whoa." Ian grabbed her arm and pulled her back.

The other guys stepped aside and stared.

"Chill, Byrne," Carlyle said, both hands raised, palms up in surrender. "I didn't really say that last bit. I thought it, but ... I just added it to make the story better."

She ripped her arm free from Ian's grip. "The story sucks no matter how you tell it." Then she bolted off the elevator, hands shaking and Ian hot on her heals.

"Byrne."

"I'm fine, Pratt." She picked up her pace and ducked into the banquet room, taking a seat between Lloyd McKellar, the pitching coach, and Alex Namath, the athletic trainer.

Pratt looked her way once, concern wrinkling his face, but then he took a seat across the room. Smart man.

"How's my ace?" Coach McKellar asked.

She felt her nostrils flare. "Never better." At least she would be. She had the rest of tonight and tomorrow morning to get the crazies under control.

"You look a little tense," he said, and then he patted her on the shoulder. "You got this, kid. Just another day in the ballpark." He pushed back in his chair and headed for the freshly served buffet.

Her stomach was in knots, and she wasn't sure she could eat. Still, she went to the buffet when Coach McKellar left his chair, because she didn't want to give Ian easy access to her. Not that he looked particularly interested anymore.

Across the room, he was laughing with Sutter. That was where he belonged. Even if it annoyed her that, with everything he had going on, he could be so carefree.

Five minutes later, with a plate full of vegetables surrounding a single scoop of pasta, Pauly headed back to her table only to find Coach Slater in her seat. "Byrne, relocate. Coach Mac and I have to run over a few things."

She nodded and looked around the room. She sure as hell wasn't sitting in the thick of idiocracy on the far side, so she located Flynn, who was sitting at the U-shaped formation of tables next to Quincy Marshall and Cody Becker. There was an open seat among them. Unfortunately, the seat put her facing Carlyle and within earshot of his motor mouth.

"And then Pratt planted his hands on the top of the keg and lifted himself into a handstand. Fucking epic. You remember that?"

If Ian responded, she didn't hear. She chewed a forkful of pasta and glanced across the table, past Becker, using her hair as a privacy curtain. Ian was smiling in Carlyle's direction, but it wasn't his usual wattage.

"You're not eating much," Flynn said.

She nodded. "Nerves."

"Is your dad making the trip?" Quincy asked her.

"He is." *Because he was laid off.* The thought ratcheted up her anxiety.

She should've pushed the destructive thoughts out of her head. Used the tools she'd cultivated all these years. At least kept her focus on Quincy, who was seated beside Becker. But, instead, she let her brain rattle on as she kept one ear on the ruckus at the back table.

"What if you pitch again in Arlington? Will he make that trip, too?" Becker asked.

"Yep."

Flynn leaned in and brushed his shoulder against hers. "Are you sure it's just nerves?"

Carlyle's laugh assaulted her ears. "When did you become a fucking monk?"

Pretty much everyone in the room looked at the back table after that.

Carlyle must've sensed he was the center of attention, because he raised his voice when he said, "Pratt doesn't drink anymore. Can you believe that?"

"And he's celibate," Sanchez added.

They were all laughing now—except for her and Flynn and probably Fry and maybe a handful of other guys who didn't give a shit about Pratt's sexcapades.

"Just cutting back," Ian said, his attention on his plate.

She cringed. She didn't want to care about any of this, but she did. She doubted Ian had told those guys about his father, which made Carlyle screwing with him about not drinking especially shitty.

"Byrne." Flynn nudged her. "Are you okay?"

She nodded, but she didn't take her ears off the back corner.

"Nobody willingly cuts back," Carlyle said.

"Maybe he drank too much and forgot to bag it," Sanchez said. "Maybe there's a mini Pratt growing in some babe's belly."

Her stomach rolled, and she pushed her plate away.

"Not even close," Ian said.

"He just realized he needed to sober up to actually catch the ball," Caceres said, adding a quick, "I'm just kidding, man."

But there was an angry tick in Ian's jaw.

Why didn't he say something? He didn't have to spill about his dad, but he could quip back and shut them up.

Across the table from Pauly, Becker said, "My mom's coming to Arlington. I told her it was a wasted trip, because I won't get in unless something happens to Pratt, but she wants to be there."

"My mom, too," Quincy said. "And there's not a shot in hell I'm getting in."

The guys laughed, and Pauly strained to hear Carlyle.

"Seriously, this alcohol-free shit better end soon," he said. "If you're not getting drunk and stupid, I'm not getting any new material. There's a whole HBO special inside you, man."

Pauly sat back and glared at Carlyle. How bad would it be if she went at him again? Clocked him good so he shut his mouth once and for all? Somebody needed to defend Ian. And just like that, Ian connected with her, making eye contact that caused a spark. A fleeting smile touched his lips and settled her racing heart. For a minute.

"I'm just glad you're not really celibate," Carlyle said, and Ian looked away from her. "Some of the best stories come from your hookups."

"You're really starting to worry me," Flynn said in her ear.

"Is she flying or driving?" Quincy asked.

"Driving with my stepdad," Becker said.

Pauly wondered if this was what it felt like to be schizophrenic. So many voices, no way to shut them off, and a building sense of dread.

"Remember that time in Asheville?" The minute Carlyle asked it, Ian shook his head. It was the kind of headshake you made when you were trying to stop someone from saying something incriminating. But that didn't stop Carlyle. "You called down to the front desk to ask for more towels, and you wound up getting your knob polished by the front-desk chick instead?"

A freight train roared through Pauly's head, carrying with it a few choice words, leading them straight out of her mouth. "Carlyle, shut the fuck up!"

The room went dead. Everybody stared at her. Including Ian. She didn't care. Something needed to be said. Somebody needed to say it. And now that it was done, she pushed her chair away from the table and stood confidently.

"Headache," she said to Flynn and the others. "I need to get some rest." After she left them, she hunted down Coach Slater. "I'm not feeling well, Skip."

He looked concerned.

"Just my head," she said. "I need some quiet."

"I'll check on you later," he said. "Text if you need anything."

What she needed was to go back to before Ian Pratt mattered—when baseball didn't feel like it was slipping through her fingers.

Chapter Twelve

After all the crap Carlyle had said, Ian expected Pauly wouldn't want to see him, but he knocked on her hotel-room door anyway. When she didn't answer, he knocked again, leaning his shoulder against the wood and putting his mouth close to the jamb.

"It's me. Open up, please."

"Go away." She sounded close, like she was pressed against the door, too.

He laid his hand on the cool surface and imagined connecting with her. "Pauly, talk to me. Is this about the shit Carlyle was saying? Because you're right. He's a fucking idiot. Half of his stories aren't even true. Or they're crazy embellished. The front desk chick didn't—"

The door flung open with a violent swing, and Ian tumbled into the room. "Shut up!" She pushed past him for a quick look up and down the hall. "What if someone hears you?"

"Hears me what? Apologizing for the crap you had to overhear?"

She yanked him completely into her room—none too friendly—and closed the door. "Don't you get it? That makes us look guilty. Why would you apologize or explain yourself to me when you couldn't even defend yourself to half the team downstairs?"

They were toe to toe, and when she stopped for a noisy inhale, her breasts brushed his chest. He wanted her. In every way possible. But right now, he wanted to figure out what was causing this meltdown so he could get her back on track.

"That's why you're mad? Because I didn't say something to shut him up downstairs?"

"Yes." She blinked. "No." She blinked again. "I don't know. I'm just losing it, and you ..." She poked him in the pec. "You aren't helping. You let them laugh at you like you're this jerk who only cares about getting drunk and getting laid." She looked at him like she was trying to get him to understand something she didn't even fully comprehend, and it unnerved him.

He stared back with the same intensity. "Because that's the guy they see," he said.

"Then show them someone else." He didn't recall her taking a step forward, but they were even closer now. Her palm flattened on his chest, and her body grazed his, kicking his pulse into high gear. "You haven't had a drink in almost a month, and unless you've been kissing somebody else, I know you're not getting laid, either. That guy they were talking about downstairs doesn't exist anymore."

"Because of you." He gathered her hand in his and held it over his heart. "*You* make me better." And then he went and proved that wrong by slipping a hand to the back of her neck and pulling her in for a kiss.

He didn't know what compelled him to wrap his arm around her waist and eliminate the air between them. He just knew he needed her to understand how much he needed her.

For too long, her lips were still, so he tried harder. He tugged gently on her hair, willing her to open. He sucked her bottom lip, desperate for a reaction. Finally, with a whimper, she surrendered, fisting his T-shirt in her hands and opening her mouth to tangle with his tongue. Relief swept through him along with a desire so wild it shook the ground where he stood.

He stumbled backward, deeper into the room, lost in her mouth, taking her with him. He shoved his hands beneath her shirt to explore the smooth skin on her back, the bumps along her spine, and the nip of her waist. His hands fit perfectly there.

"We shouldn't do this here," she said, pulling back. Her breath was warm on his face, and her lids were heavy over her eyes. She looked like she wanted—no, *needed*—to be kissed again, but after that declaration, he didn't dare.

He lightened his grip on her waist and bit his cheek for a reality check. "Then we won't."

She frowned, closed her eyes, and ran hands down his front. "But I want to. So bad." She was sexy as hell, struggling with her demons. "I *need* to. I need something to release all this pressure."

He nearly groaned. "Then we will."

A second later, the backs of his legs hit the bed, and he pulled her down on top of him. They didn't miss a beat, kissing and pawing at clothing until they were both shirtless. She grazed fingernails down his chest and then rose up to unhook her bra. *Christ*, she was amazing. He was a goner before she ever settled her bottom against the ridge in his jeans and leaned forward to offer him a beautiful, brown nipple. He took every bit of flesh she offered. Licking and sucking. Touching and teasing. Until her rocking and bouncing threatened to make him come in his pants.

"Pauly," he growled, gripping her backside to hold her still.

"Ian," she whispered against his ear, teasing him with her tongue as she traveled down his neck.

He lifted his chin with a gruff noise of appreciation, and she kissed him there, brushed her lips over the lump in his throat, just barely dragged her teeth along his clavicle. "See? I feel better already," she said, her hand snaking up his side, making him shiver, and he could almost feel her smiling against his skin.

In a flash, she scooted down his legs and sat back on his knees, working on loosening his jeans. Her hair fell forward, blocking most of her face, but he could still see her parted lips and feel each exhale on his stomach. *Damn.* At this rate, it would be over the second she got her hands on him.

Ian tugged on her arms and rolled them over so he was above her.

She was laughing with her mouth and eyes, her hair spiraling out around her. He kissed her until she quieted. "It's not nice to laugh at a man when you're driving him crazy."

She cupped his face and stared up at him. "I like driving you crazy."

"Yeah?" He grabbed her wrists and pulled her hands from his face, pinning them above her head. "Let's see how much you like it now." He dragged his mouth along the sensitive underside of her arm and heard her sharp intake of breath. With his thumb, he traced the seam of her jeans. She arched against his hand, but the rest of her tensed. Always aiming for control.

Tonight, he was going to shatter that.

He took her breast in his mouth again and rolled his tongue around her nipple until she moaned. One more sweep, and she lowered her hands, unbuttoning and unzipping her jeans.

"I was going to do that," he said.

"Then why didn't you?" She wiggled beneath him, shimmying out of the denim even as his hand worked past her panties. "You're slow, Pratt." His name came on a hiss as his thumb slid between her slick folds.

"You'll thank me for that later."

She whimpered and let her legs widen.

He shifted his weight to the mattress beside her, watching the muscles in her face relax, getting off on the curves and sharp edges of her body. He could've stayed like that all night, touching her, teasing her, taking in every part—but *damn it*, she tried to speed things up again with a hand on his distended fly.

He hissed in a breath and moved out of reach, kissing the inside of her knee and up her thigh, until the scent of her arousal made his mouth water. But he pulled back, prolonging the game.

"Oh my gawd!" She ground the words out, and he smiled.

"You like that?"

"I'd like it better if you just finished me."

He laughed, his gaze skimming her body until he reached her face. "Relax, Byrne. Unlike you, I play all nine innings."

Her head shot up, eyes open. "I can pitch a full game."

"Can you?" He slid a finger inside of her and watched the shock and pleasure register on her face. Then, slowly, achingly, he lowered his mouth. "Let's find out."

The tip of his tongue met her soft flesh. One flick. Two. He moved his finger inside of her, but not too deep. Her hands wound in the bedding beside her, and she made soft noises that tightened his balls. If getting her off was this good, getting him off was going to be insane.

And then, in an instant, their world rattled.

Someone was knocking on the door.

• • •

Pauly bolted out from underneath Ian. Sheer terror twisted the muscles in her face to the point of pain.

"Fuck," she mouthed.

Ian didn't look as rattled. And, damn him, he still exuded sex as he stood there shirtless, handing over her jeans. She needed more than her bottom covered in denim. She needed a lobotomy.

Shit. She snatched his T-shirt off the floor because it was within reach and pulled it over her head.

"Byrne, it's Coach Slater." He knocked again. "Just want to make sure you're okay."

Since she didn't have to look through the peephole to see who it was, she simply dropped her forehead to the door and wished the earth would open up and swallow her whole.

"Hey, Skip. I'm good." But her inhale was shaky. "I just got out of the shower. I'm literally"—she glanced down at Ian's Aces

T-shirt, complete with his number below her left breast and its still-hardened nipple—"not decent. Otherwise, I would open the door. But I promise. I'm good." Just completely out of control.

"Okay. Do you need anything?" he asked. "Buzz does that manipulation thingy on necks. It works like magic on headaches."

"No, thanks." She didn't need anybody else's hands on her tonight.

"Then I'll check on you again at curfew."

She rolled her back to the door and stared at Ian. He sat on the end of the bed, legs spread, palms pressed into the mattress behind him. Shirtless. Like he had every right and reason to be in her room.

And, God help her, she smelled like him, covered in draping cotton that had clung to his body before they'd lost their minds.

He looked over his shoulder and then back at her with a wicked spark in his eyes. "It's your call, but we still have two hours until curfew."

She gaped, pushed off the door, and shook her head wildly. "No. You need to leave."

"Right now?"

"Right now." She whipped his T-shirt over her head and threw it at him. It dropped at his feet, and he took forever to pick it up, probably because he was too damn busy looking at her breasts. "Get out."

"Okay. Okay." Every muscle he owned flexed as he stood and worked his way into the shirt.

He was as mouthwatering as he was maddening. And despite the horribly compromising position they'd just been in, her body was primed for more of it.

She scrambled for her clothes, ducking out of self-preservation when she passed him. "Please, hurry."

He caught her by the waist at the exact moment she grabbed her shirt. And somehow, she managed to line up all the holes with the right body parts as he hauled her to stand. "No harm, no foul," he said, his hands on her skin, obstructing her shirt. "Don't freak out about this. He doesn't know I'm in here."

"But *I* know." She wrenched his hands from her waist. "And I know what we almost did—on team time."

Ian grinned. "I don't see the problem. You said you *needed* it."

She groaned in frustration. "That just makes it worse. I was out of my mind, and I can't be out of my mind. I pitch tomorrow. I need consistency to go out there and do what I do. This is not going to help me get control."

"Hey." He slid a hand up her arm, and she cursed her traitorous body for relishing every goose pimple. "You're an amazing woman and an amazing pitcher. I've seen what you can do. Don't sell yourself short. You can have everything you want, Pauly. Everything. You deserve it, too."

Oh, God. He was smooth. But he was just trying to get her back into bed, wasn't he? Maybe the baby blues and the killer charm were exactly how he'd ended up with more than towels from some front-desk clerk. But that didn't feel right, either. Because honesty shone in Ian's eyes, and Pauly wanted to believe him. She wanted to believe she could claim a man and a career in baseball, but she knew better. Her entire life had been an uphill battle, where day in and day out, she needed to prove she belonged on the same field as the boys. What would sleeping with one in the middle of a championship series prove?

"I can't." She backed away. "I have to be ready for tomorrow."

The sincerity in his eyes morphed into something that looked a lot like determination. "You will be." Then he planted an oddly platonic kiss on the center of her forehead and walked to the door.

The deep sense of panic she'd felt right before she'd stepped on the elevator returned. She might be losing her mind, but she didn't want to lose him completely.

"Ian," she blurted. "I don't want anything to change between us."

"It won't." He smiled reassuringly, and then his eyebrow quirked. "Now, put on your pants."

She looked down at her bare legs and scrambled into her jeans. The last thing she needed was someone walking by and seeing her pantless as he left her room.

But he didn't leave.

He opened the door, shoved the desk chair beneath the knob, and left them exposed.

She ducked out of view. "What are you doing?"

"Insurance," he said, then he smoothed out the wrinkles they'd made in the bedspread and sat in a nearby chair. "Get your laptop."

"Why?"

"So I can help you get ready for tomorrow."

"Ian, I don't think—"

He shushed her. "The door's open, *Byrne*. Be careful how loudly you protest. People might get the wrong idea about us." He grinned.

She was vibrating with a combination of annoyance, nerves, and some leftover lust thrown in for good measure. "I can get ready on my own, you know. I usually do."

"Fine. Then I'll leave." He grabbed the armrests and lifted off the chair, and in that fraction of a second, she didn't want him to go. She wanted someone to get ready with, someone who knew her strengths and weaknesses—on and off the field.

She was just totally blown away by the fact that that someone was Ian.

• • •

Pauly squeaked out the win on Sunday, and Ian couldn't have been happier if she'd pitched a perfect game. Knowing what she'd been through the night before—what she'd had to work through to be composed on the mound—made him respect her even more. She was a smart, fierce, sexy competitor. And he liked watching her soar.

He caught up with her in the hotel lobby and pulled her by the strap of her duffle bag into the hotel gym.

"What?" she asked sharply, but there was a smile in her eyes.

"Did you want to thank me now?"

She smirked. "Pratt, we may have won, but I walked three batters and gave up two runs. That's a substandard day's work in my book. Besides, there's a wall of windows behind you."

He glanced behind him and saw clean through to the front desk. *Shit.* "Must've been blinded by your beauty when I dragged you in here."

"Smooth talker."

"I'm smooth at a lot of things."

"Don't." She held up a hand and backed toward the door, her eyes shining, her lips quirking.

"Don't what?"

"Don't get me started."

"You mean don't rev you up and turn you on."

She nodded madly. "Yes, that."

"You know you're going to have to kiss me again before you pitch again."

"I might not pitch again."

"Then you're going to have to kiss me again just because you want to. Like you did last night."

"Ian," she said, low and breathy, and if it hadn't been for those damn windows, he would've kissed her right then up against the door.

"Just tell me you want to kiss me again, and I'll be satisfied."

Her brows lifted. "Really?"

"No, but I'll pretend to be."

She laughed, and the whole world brightened.

"I think you pitched a great game today," he said. "I'm proud of you."

"I'm proud of you, too."

"For what?"

But then her eyes slid away from his face to the windows behind him. "Crap. I gotta go."

She was out of the gym before he could blink.

Instead of following her, Ian turned and watched her race across the lobby to three men. They were equally big and equally dark-skinned. From the way she embraced them soundly, Ian figured they were family. And if he wasn't mistaken, the older gentleman had an eye on him.

The slightly taller of the two younger men flung an arm around Pauly's shoulder and led her away. The other guy followed, but the older man stayed. And, again, Ian could've sworn the man was looking in his direction.

Ian shrugged off his paranoia and pushed out of the gym. A few steps down the hall, the man reappeared.

"Where ya headed, son?" His words were friendly enough, but his tone was distant.

"No place special," Ian said.

"Good. Can I have a minute of your time?"

"Sure."

The man led Ian to a table in the lobby, where they sat and looked each other over.

"Do you know who I am?" the man finally asked.

"I'm assuming you're Pauly Byrne's dad."

The man nodded. "And you're her catcher. Ian Pratt. Played some small college club ball. Rode the pine until Tuck Mason's luck ran out. Cuts grass on the side. Got off to a shaky start with my daughter. How am I doin'?"

Shit, the man knew a lot about him. "Good," Ian said, a little scared.

"Good. Ya see, I don't miss much, and I don't miss anything where my daughter is concerned. She said you've been able to work through some things and you've been helping her find her rhythm on the field, so I wanted to offer my thanks." He reached a massive hand across the table.

"Just doing my job," Ian said, hesitating on the handshake. But he didn't want to be rude, either, so he took a breath and raised his hand.

The shake was rough. A nonverbal warning. *I'm watching you, and if you screw up, I'll snap you in half.* Ian got the message loud and clear.

Thank God he hadn't done something stupid like kiss Pauly in the gym in front of a wall of windows. In front of her father.

Or Ian would be dead by now.

Chapter Thirteen

The Aces dropped the next game in Urbana. Fry's start was solid, and the relievers did their best, but all it took was one fluke long ball and a shutout from the Undertakers' pitching staff to send the Aces back to Arlington with the championship series tied 1-1.

Of course, Pauly's dad was thrilled, and secretly Pauly saw it as a blessing, too. With Tuesday being a travel day and Wednesday night being Game Three, Pauly was poised to start Game Four on Thursday. It was the best-case scenario for her career. From a scouting perspective, all eyes were on the last two teams standing. She would love nothing better than to have to withdraw her name from contention for the coaching position because she'd been picked up by a minor-league team.

"Your dad's an intimidating man," Ian said.

Ian was sitting across the table from Pauly in a booth at Denny's on Tuesday night, two hours after they'd arrived back in Arlington. His Aces sweatshirt was unzipped, revealing a soft-looking, snug-fitting white T-shirt. And all Pauly wanted to do was strip him bare and forget about everything else.

That was the problem. The wanting was driving them to take unnecessary risks, like the interaction her father had witnessed in the hotel gym. That had to be why he'd cornered Ian.

"He's just keeping my best interests at heart," she said. "As long as I'm winning, he should behave."

Ian pretended to choke on his banana split. "Keep winning, babe. Otherwise, I'm afraid he'll kill me."

She laughed. "You're off the hook for tonight. He stopped in Columbus, at the Football Hall of Fame, so you can relax. He's not going to pop up outside this window."

Ian wiped a hand across his forehead in feigned relief and smiled brightly. "So you're free tonight?"

"No." She grinned when his smile faltered. "I'm with you."

"Excellent."

"But no sex," she said, leaning across the table to guard her words.

He gave her one of those looks that said he could change her mind. "You know, this is all just foreplay. You *need* it, Byrne. Bad. I can see it in your eyes. You're going to crack one of these days." He sat back, eating his ice cream, as innocent as can be, but under the table, his foot skimmed the inside of her leg.

She laughed again. "That doesn't work."

"Why not?"

"Because you're wearing sneakers and your feet are too big. That's clunky, not sexy."

"Maybe I'm just doing it wrong. Maybe I need a lesson. If you're such an expert, show me."

"Who said I'm an expert?"

"I thought you said you were good at everything you do."

"Honey, I'm better than good." She toed off her running shoe and rubbed the arch of her foot over the thin fabric of his track pants, up and down, higher and higher, watching his eyes glaze over and his facial muscles go slack. When she reached his knee and zeroed in on his groin, he caught her foot in his hands.

Ian smiled wickedly. "Trick play." His voice was rough as he pressed his thumb into the ball of her foot. He circled, rubbed, and pressed until she leaned back, closed her eyes, and felt breathless.

"I'm going to miss you so much," she said mindlessly.

He stopped rubbing and stared at her. "Where are you going?"

"Well, I don't know." She tried to laugh it off. "But this is temporary. Right? All of it is temporary."

His eyes darkened, and he frowned.

She wanted to pull them out of this tight spot, so she kept talking. "I still could end up in the minors. Or in New Jersey. I have an interview in September."

"Coaching shouldn't even be an option after the way you've been pitching."

"I know, but as long as my dad's not working, it has to be an option. Besides, it's a great opportunity."

"Just because it's a great opportunity doesn't mean it's the right opportunity."

His words reminded her of something similar Tyler had said, when she'd told him she was going to get past her disappointment over not being drafted by trying out for the Aces. But Tyler had been wrong then. The Aces ended up being both a great opportunity and the right opportunity. Maybe Ian was wrong now. Maybe Holymount was the right choice for her, too.

She pulled her foot from his hand.

"Can I get you two anything else?" the waiter asked.

Another season, Pauly thought.

But Ian shook his head.

Which was the right answer to everything. This couldn't go on much longer without something bad happening. Still, she let herself indulge.

Outside in the parking lot, she wiggled against him when he backed her against her car.

"You don't start tomorrow," he said. "Why don't we go back to your place and have a little fun?"

"But *you* start tomorrow," she said, winding her arms beneath his sweatshirt and raising her mouth to his. "Your head should be focused on baseball."

"One of them is," he said with a smile a second before they kissed.

They stayed like that, mildly making out against a parked car at the dark edge of a Denny's lot, long enough for the temperature to drop and Ian to wrap her in his sweatshirt. And then he tucked her in her car and sent her home.

Her insides were a total mess. She'd never felt this way before. Not even with Tyler. And she'd thought she'd loved him. *Shit.*

Pauly shut down. She refused to admit the obvious. Admitting it would just make things worse. There was no future here—with or without Ian. She was either going to make it to the minors, or she was going to end up in Holymount.

An hour later, she curled up in bed, dressed in her PJs and Ian's sweatshirt, wondering if there really was a way she could have everything.

The next morning, she was startled awake by pounding on her door. For one groggy second, she thought she was back in Urbana with Ian in her hotel room and Coach Slater about to bust them.

Of course, it wasn't Coach Slater this time. It was her dad.

"It's 7:30 in the morning," she said, blinking the sleep from her eyes, trying to contain her worry. "What are you doing here? I thought you were in Columbus."

"I drove all night." He sounded strangely agitated as he pushed into her apartment.

His gaze swept over her, landing on the sweatshirt that hung large and limp on her body. His eyes zeroed in on Ian's number. Then he looked around the apartment, *thoroughly*, making her stomach sink.

She tried not to let it visibly shake her. "Dad, what's going on?"

"I got a call yesterday, tipping me off to a blog post."

"What blog post?"

He hesitated. "I wasn't sure I was doing the right thing telling you this the day before a start, but ..." He eyed the sweatshirt again. "You need to know. We can work through the fallout together."

"What the heck?" She wrapped the fleece taut around her body. "You're scaring me."

"Some Holymount players and parents have banded together to protest the university's willingness to interview you for the coaching position."

"Why?"

"Because you're a woman. Why else?"

All these years, and it was always the same damn thing.

"I know what an internet hound you are, so I figured it would be useless trying to hide it. If sports radio picks it up, it could go national."

"What'd the post say?"

"The concerned individuals believe hiring a woman to coach young men will blur lines and cause an unnecessary distraction."

"Typical." And disappointing.

"The anonymous blogger claims to have the support of twenty players and their families."

"Twenty?" Her voice cracked with disbelief. "That's more than half the roster."

"And supposedly the College Player of the Year has threatened to transfer if you're hired, because he respects his mama, and she's worried you're going to have inappropriate interactions with her son."

Again, her father's gaze fled her face and lowered over the sweatshirt.

Pauly was too angry at the injustice to worry about what he was thinking. "You can't be serious."

"I'm dead serious."

"That's ridiculous."

"Is it? Because that goddamn sweatshirt has me worried now."

"Then don't look at it," she said, her voice coming out with an edge. "It's not the issue here, and you know it."

Her father shook his head. "You gotta be shittin' me with this right now, P." He crossed his arms and stared at her intensely.

"Kid, this is your career we're talking about. Everything you've worked for your whole damn life. What happened to never letting a guy make you look stupid again? Isn't that what you told me after Tyler?"

"Ian's not making me look stupid," she snapped. "In fact, I look fabulous." She straightened her shoulders and tempered her tone. This conversation was probably long overdue, considering life after baseball would most certainly mean life without her father—and mother—so intimately involved in her business, but she didn't want her words to come between them. "Dad, if you want to talk about my career right now, fine. Let's talk about it. I'm pitching better than I have all season. But I'm not going to talk to you about my personal life."

He stared at her for a beat, his face unreadable, and then he nodded, as something akin to relief washed over his face. "You're pitching great this season, P."

"Thank you."

"I just don't like it when people talk shit about you, and I don't want you giving them ammunition."

"People have been talking shit about me since I picked up a baseball. I'm used to it."

"I'm not."

His protective streak had provided the most generous safety net when she was forging her way through boys' baseball, but she didn't need it anymore.

"Dad, it's all going to be okay." She was going to win a championship. He was going to find another job. And she was going to make it to the minors. This crap about the blog post made her want it even more. "Every shitty thing they say about me is just fuel for the fire. You taught me that."

He smiled. "I did."

"You taught me a lot of things, and I'm grateful, but I'm learning a lot on my own, now, too."

"P—"

She held up her hand, needing to get it all out before she forgot the words. "I appreciate you so much. I appreciate everything you've done, but I'm not going to let my career choices suck the life out of you. I'll figure out what to do about next season on my own when the time comes. Okay? You and mom can officially stop worrying."

"We're always going to worry, P." Emotion filled his voice and glistened in his eyes, making Pauly feel a little weepy. "But maybe we could try to cheer more than we worry."

"I would like that." She held out her hand, palm up, waiting for him to join her in the victory handshake they'd created when she was a child. They carried it off with only one teensy tiny mistake.

"I'm glad we had this talk," he said.

"Me too."

She felt readier than ever to win a championship.

• • •

Wednesday morning, Ian made his way up his father's driveway to the front porch, where Aunt May sat on the swing. She greeted him with a kiss on the cheek, smelling like baby powder and cigarettes.

"Aren't you just the best-looking man I've ever seen?" She eyed him up like he was prime rib, which would've been creepy if he didn't have loads of experience with his father's colorful younger sister. May lived for Virginia Slims, Pepsi, pistachios, cats with way too much hair, and talking about "hunky" men.

"How did this happen?" she squealed. "I used to change your diaper. I've seen your peeny."

"Peeny?" Ian cringed. And since he didn't want to encourage this line of conversation, he dove right into the reason he was here. "Thank you for coming, Aunt May. I really appreciate it."

"That's what family's for." She pinched his cheek, and something flashed in her eyes, something that looked a lot like sympathy, which wasn't a bad guess, considering she'd been in Arlington before—after Ian's mother had died—to help Ray keep his head above water.

"How is he?" Ian asked.

She backed herself onto the swing and waved a hand through the air. "He's in bed. He says he feels sick. And, Lord, does he shake."

"Is that from the withdrawal? Didn't they give him meds for home?"

"He has more pills than a pharmacy, but half the time he won't take what he's 'posta. I told him he's only hurting himself, but you know Raymond. Stubborn old ass."

"I'll talk to him." Ian reached for the screen door.

"Good luck," she sang.

At least the house was clean. Aunt May might not be able to get his dad to take his meds regularly, but she certainly knew how to organize a hellhole and make it look halfway livable. It even smelled like Murphy's Oil Soap and fresh coffee instead of rotgut liquor and unwashed male.

Ian breathed deeply and headed straight for his father's bedroom, where Ray was watching *The Price Is Right* on an old twenty-inch, box TV.

"Jesus Christ," Ray said to the woman on the television. "Everybody in the damn place was yelling one dollar. Are you deaf?" He looked at Ian when he stepped into the room.

Ray's color was back. Gone was the ashy gray. And his eyes shone clear for the first time in ages. But May was right—Ray's hands shook like he had advanced Parkinson's Disease.

"Dad," Ian said, deciding to focus on the positive. "You look real good."

"That's funny. I feel like hell."

"Because you're not taking your medicine."

Ray groaned. "My sister's nothing but a snitch."

"She came all the way from Florida to clean your filthy house and get you back on track. I think that makes her a lot more than a snitch. Be nice."

Ray nodded while he thought it through. "She tell you I'm going to start AA meetings at the church as soon as I can get out of this bed?"

"No, she didn't, but that's great, Dad. And it's even more reason why you need to take your damn medicine."

Ray grimaced and pursed his lips like he had a sudden, violent case of reflux. "You can leave if you came here to yell at me."

"I didn't come here to yell. I haven't seen you in over a week. I thought we could hang out until I have to be at the field."

Ray slipped his jittery hands beneath the covers and turned his attention back to the television. "Too tired. Maybe tomorrow."

Ian tabled his disappointment. His dad was sick, not being unreasonably cruel. "I can't do tomorrow, Dad. I have another game. A big one. Tomorrow night we could be champions."

"Wish I could be there," Ray said without taking his eyes off the screen.

"Me, too." Ian stood inside the door a second longer, not knowing what he was waiting for.

"If you're hanging around hoping I'll talk to you about my money problems, you'd be better off leavin'."

As far as the foreclosures went, Ian had reached a dead end days ago when his dad was unreachable in detox. Lawyers could only do so much when a third party with limited information was the one spearheading things.

"That hadn't even crossed my mind," Ian said. He'd figured he would pick it up hard after the season was over. "But now that you mention it …"

Ray frowned. "Can't a man rest in peace?"

"Yeah. When he's dead, Dad. But you're not, so let's figure out a way to fix your financial mess now that you're sober. I left some numbers on the counter while you were in detox. Call them. Tell them who you are. They can help."

"Another time," Ray said, eyes back on the screen. It was obvious he wasn't in the mood for company, and Ian wasn't in the mood to play any games, aside from the ones on the field. "Fine," he said. "Then all you gotta do is take your medicine, and I'll leave."

Ray nodded. "You got yourself a deal."

After Ian made sure his father swallowed every pill, he returned to the front porch with two cups of coffee, one for Aunt May. She sat on the crooked porch swing, sucking on a skinny cigarette, her nostrils flaring with every inhale.

"Thank ya, hun." She took the mug in her free hand and rested it on her bony knee. "How'd he treat ya?"

"Like a sober man who doesn't wanna be sober."

She nodded. "He'll get over that. I'm not leaving 'til he does. My friend, Janice, has the cats. I told her I might not be back for a while." She raised the mug to her mouth but then lowered it an inch. "Why didn't you call me sooner and tell me things were this bad?"

"I didn't realize it myself."

"Ostrich syndrome," she said, smiling. "Just like your dad. He didn't realize how bad things were with his marriage, either, until your mother left."

The coffee went down rough, searing Ian's throat and leaving a trail of pain all the way to his belly. He didn't want to sit here and talk about his mother.

"Raymond started drinking long before that, though," May said. "You wouldn't remember a lot of the rough spots."

But Ian did, he just forced them down so deep they couldn't cause him any more pain. And that was where he wanted them to stay.

"What a pair! Ray wouldn't get help for his drinking, and Barbie wouldn't get help for her"—May pointed a finger to her temple and gave it a little whirl—"head."

And Ian stared into the bottom of his coffee cup, watching the steam curl up and disappear, just like he wanted to do.

"I don't know why anybody gets married," May continued. "Thank the good Lord, I got the memo when I was young. I got beat over the head with it." She chuckled, and it turned into a smoker's cough. When she recovered, she said, "My granddaddy was an alcoholic. Did you know that?"

"No." That revelation settled heavy in Ian's chest.

"My daddy was an alcoholic, too. His brother was an alcoholic, and my brother is an alcoholic." May pushed her feet against the porch and set the swing in motion. "*Woowee!* That's some track record. I say love of the drink just goes along with having a peeny."

Ian wished he could laugh at her awkward word choice, her nasally voice, and the way her eyes bugged out each time she lifted her legs to propel the swing, but his family history chilled him to his core.

"I didn't know all that," he said. "Dad never talks about his family."

"Would you?" She snorted a laugh. "They're all drunks, except me."

Things were way worse than Ian had imagined. He'd always believed he was just like his dad. He'd held on to that like it was a good thing, because the alternative was even bleaker. But, *Jesus*, after what he'd been through these last few weeks … It was a tossup: staring down the bottom of a vodka bottle or the barrel of a gun.

"Anyway, it looks like you got the memo, too." May went right on talking and swinging, oblivious to Ian's torment. "Considering your gene pool, that's a good thing. Less casualties." She dragged on her cigarette, sucking so hard he imagined the inside of her cheeks meeting in the middle of her mouth. "Who was that nice girl you used to date?"

"Sara," he said without thought, feeling numb.

"What's she up to these days?"

"Married with kids."

May laughed until it turned into another cough, then she said, "Looks like she didn't get the memo."

Ian sat back and took in his surroundings. The rickety, peeling porch. The dusty, barren lawn. The mechanic's garage with a hole in the roof. All of it about to be bank owned. And why not? Who the hell else would want it? There was a reason people drank. To forget about how shitty life could be. To stop being a sad sack and smile once in a while.

The only smiling he'd done in the last thirty days—without a drink—was aimed at Pauly. And that was just another addiction waiting to happen.

If he thought for a minute he could actually be the right man for a woman like Pauly Byrne, he was crazier than his mother had ever been.

His phone vibrated, startling him. The group text he'd jokingly named "numbnutz" after a particularly rowdy night, lit up with messages from Carlyle, Sanchez, and Martinez.

Carlyle: Foley's after the game?

Sanchez: In.

Martinez: In.

Ian's thumb hovered over the phone, ready to beg off. But he could already taste the hops and barley on his tongue, the rowdy noise of the bar crowding out all the depressing thoughts of foreclosures and medicine.

Carlyle: Cool. Pratt? You coming or you still being a little bitch?

He swallowed hard. Why fight it? You could only do so much to delay destiny. Ian set his jaw and typed back:

I'm in too.

Chapter Fourteen

Pauly arrived at the stadium fifteen minutes before call time instead of her usual thirty minutes, which was her personal rule on days when she was scheduled to start. Since Boardman would take the mound tonight in Game Three, the pressure was off her.

After she changed into her team-issued workout gear, she headed to the field for stretches.

"Ace," Sutter called down the hall, tipping his hat to her.

She smiled, nodded, and caught up with him outside the clubhouse entrance. "What's up, Sutter?" They bumped fists and clamped hands.

"Nothing much. Just working on winning a championship." He winked.

She smiled, and they walked onto the field together. "I have a good feeling about this series."

"Me, too," he said.

Sanchez jogged up beside her. "Wish you could pitch every game, Ace."

Which didn't reflect nicely on Boardman, but Pauly appreciated the sentiment. "I wish I could, too. Not sure how long my arm would hold up, though."

They shared a laugh. Their little group expanded to include Flynn, Caceres, and Fry. But no Pratt. She tried not to obsess about that. She wasn't his keeper. She wasn't even his girlfriend. Although, she'd been thinking about that a lot since the conversation with her father. Maybe after they won this championship, she would rethink the no-labels thing.

She settled in the infield grass amid small talk and teasing with her teammates. These were her favorite moments, when all that mattered was baseball, and she was just one of the guys.

"You coming out with us tonight?" Sanchez asked.

Pauly shook her head. "I start tomorrow."

"Respect," he said, pounding his chest a couple times, then he directed the question at Sutter and the rest of the crew, "How 'bout you guys? Positive visualization and all that. We're gonna win, so we need to plan to celebrate."

Sutter chuckled. "I'll celebrate when we actually win the championship."

Flynn and Fry begged off for family reasons.

"Caceres, come on," Sanchez said. "I know you got a ball and chain now, but Pratt's back in on this one, too."

Pauly leaned forward into a calf stretch and tried to hide her skepticism. She wanted to argue with Sanchez. No way was Ian going out drinking. But she kept her mouth shut and told herself it was just Sanchez's wishful thinking.

Pratt finally showed up about ten minutes into stretches. She didn't like that he was late—it smacked of old Ian—but she didn't know exactly where he'd been. For all she knew, he could've been tied up talking to Coach in the clubhouse, which meant he wasn't technically late at all. Regardless, she didn't need to be keeping tabs on him.

After a little strength training and some throws to Becker in the bullpen, Pauly's non-start pregame ritual was complete, and she headed back to the clubhouse for a recovery shake before she would head back to the bullpen to watch the game.

She saw Ian by his locker, fumbling with his mitt.

"Loose lace?" she asked, laughing at the way it sounded like a tongue twister.

"Yeah, but I got it." He didn't smile.

"You okay?"

"Fine," he said, glancing up once—and very quickly.

He didn't seem fine to her.

"How's your dad?" she asked, her voice lower now.

"Miserable," he said.

That explained his mood. "Hey." She touched his arm briefly, willing to risk any speculation from the other guys in the room if it settled him down before the game. "Whatever it is, you need to shake it off and be ready for this."

He looked at her, a hint of coldness in his eyes. "Some things can't be shaken off just like that, Byrne."

"I disagree. You're the master of your thoughts. Get control of those, and you'll be golden."

He scoffed. "I wish it was that easy. I really do."

"What's going on? Tell me. I can help you."

"I don't think you can."

She was a little hurt and a lot confused. Something had definitely happened with his father, but they didn't have nearly enough time to unpack it all before Boardman threw the first pitch. "Okay then, help yourself," she said, wanting him to know he had more power than he gave himself credit for.

But he made a sour face that said her words weren't appreciated.

"Ready, Pratt?"

Boardman stood near them with his mouth full of sunflower seeds and his mitt under his arm. And just like that, Ian left her. She tried not to make it personal.

Thankfully, Boardman and the bullpen pitched clean, and the Aces' bats were on fire, giving them the win. But Pratt bobbled a couple catches, missed another entirely, and let a runner reach first on an uncaught strike three.

She set out to talk to him again after the game, but the clubhouse was hopping, and all she could manage was a quick, "Shake it off." Followed by a playful, "We won, didn't we?" And, "Tomorrow is another game."

He met her smile with a quick smile of his own, but it was missing its usual luster. At that point, she decided to give him space. That's what she would've wanted. She would catch up with her family in the rotunda and text Ian later to make sure everything was okay. Less than twenty-four hours before a start as big as tomorrow's start, she didn't need to be worrying about him. Rest and calm were the keys to her game.

Forty-five minutes later, she walked into the first of two adjoining hotel rooms.

"Are you hungry?" her mother asked. "There's leftover chicken in the mini-fridge."

"I'm good," Pauly said as the younger of her two brothers, Devon, pushed past her to claim the leftovers.

Trey, the oldest, walked ahead, grabbed the remote, and sprawled across the nearest double bed.

ESPN wasn't on for more than five seconds when their father yelled from the bathroom, "Shut it off!"

Trey bitched and moaned. "They aren't even talking about baseball."

"ESPN won't be talking about the Aces," Pauly said, as she sat on the end of the bed.

Devon cradled the foam container of chicken against his belly and propped up against the headboard. "That's not what he's worried about."

It dawned on Pauly slowly. "Holymount?" Would ESPN talk about the blog post?

"Trey," their mother said, cool, calm, and eerily authoritarian. "Shut it off."

He did—with an eye roll—and a minute later, their father charged into the room with a murderous expression on his face. He took one look at the television and visibly relaxed.

"Dad," Pauly said, standing. "I don't mind it being on. It's all good." She couldn't hide from everything. When he looked at her, she added, "*I'm* good." And she infused that with an expression that was meant to remind him of that morning's conversation.

Her father gripped her by the shoulders. "You're better than good, P." His sharp gaze reached deep inside of her. "You're great. Legendary." He smiled. "How's that for cheerleading?"

"Perfect." Pauly hugged him. Then, she flopped onto the bed next to Devon, who'd taken time off from his job in sports marketing with the Orioles to be at these last few games. "Is it possible for us to talk about something other than baseball?" she asked.

Trey, whose promising baseball career had been derailed by chronic shoulder injuries in college, snorted. "Sure, we can."

"What do you wanna talk about?" Devon asked.

"How was the Hall of Fame?"

Trey made a low noise in his throat. "Short."

"We left after Dad found out about the blog post," Devon said.

Trey reached for the remote and turned on the television again. Pauly had no doubt he intended on channel surfing, but the sound of ESPN filled the room, and their father attacked.

"I said shut that damn thing off. She needs to stay calm." He snatched the remote out of Trey's hand and carried it with him into the other room.

"How 'bout *he* stays calm?" Devon said under his breath and around a mouthful of chicken.

"I can't stay here for the rest of the night." Trey pushed off the bed and stood. "Anybody want to walk to the bar across the street?"

Foley's. This late on a Wednesday night, it shouldn't be packed. Maybe it would be a nice change of pace. They could shoot some pool and laugh a little.

"I'll go," she said, "but I can't be out too late."

"*Shiiiit.*" Trey pointed to the room behind them. "That man'll have a search party out if you're gone past an hour."

Devon chuckled. "Who's gonna tell him we're taking his million-dollar baby to a bar?"

The guys looked at Pauly. "You're both pathetic," she said, laughing.

When the three of them walked into the adjoining room, their mother looked up from her iPad, and their father looked up from his laptop.

"We're going out for a little bit," Pauly said.

"Out where?" he asked.

"We'll keep her chill," Devon butted in.

"Out where?" he asked again, sterner this time.

"Down the street to play pool," Pauly said. "And we'll be back in an hour or two, so I can get plenty of sleep." She smiled confidently. "I know the drill, Dad. I've been doing this for years."

Ten minutes later, Pauly rolled into Foley's with her brothers on either side of her. They were laughing at the size of the town and the way some of the older people looked at them funny.

"We ain't in Baltimore anymore," Trey teased.

Pauly's laughter cut off on an intake of air when she saw who was sitting at the bar. *Ian.* Wearing a shitty-ass grin and some blonde on his lap.

Heat rushed her face, and her heart lodged in her throat. She'd been played.

Uh-uh. She was not doing this now. She spun toward the door.

"Whoa." Devon caught her by the arm. "What the hell?"

Why? Why was this happening twenty-four hours before the biggest game of her career? And how could Ian go anywhere near a bar after everything they'd been through? Just days after his father was released from detox. What was so bad it had pushed him here? His dad? The game? Or had he just been lying this whole time, kissing her against parked cars and sending her home so he could head off to Foley's?

Confusion gave way to anger, heart-pumping, fist-clenching anger.

"Motherfucker," she said.

"Who? Me?" Trey backed up.

When Devon didn't move out of her way, she pushed him aside, her eyes never leaving Pratt's big, fat head.

"Hey!" she called out when she was still a good yard away from the mostly empty bar.

Ian faced her, and at least that stupid grin died. But, a second later, he'd recovered with something more distant in its place. "Byrne," he said smoothly, dryly. "I didn't expect to see you here."

See her? He couldn't even make eye contact, and that was a shame, because she wanted to rip those pretty blue eyes right out of his head.

"I could say the same thing to you," she snapped.

"The guys have been missing me." He tossed his head in the direction of the rowdy crew around the pool tables. "Figured I owed them one."

The pretty woman on his lap sipped her beer while she studied Pauly overtop the rim. Pauly almost said, *Don't worry. I'm not a threat to whatever you two have planned*, but she couldn't stop staring at the other full glass of beer on the bar in front of Ian.

He was fucking up everything.

Caught between tears and rage, she hissed, "Why are you doing this?"

His face twisted, and he didn't look all that sure. He seemed caught between guilt and something darker, radiating from deep within him. Partly confused, partly apathetic, and crushingly like his father. "I told you some things couldn't be shaken off, but you wouldn't listen." He threw her words back at her like they'd been an insult instead of a source of encouragement.

She lunged at him. Ian flinched, and the woman jumped off his lap, but it wasn't necessary. Trey caught Pauly from behind, limiting her forward motion.

"It's over, Pratt. I don't care what you do. Just stay the fuck away from me off the field. And on it, you better be goddamned perfect, or …" She reached for the first words that popped into her head. "I'll kill you."

"Whoa," Trey said. "He's not worth it."

But he was, and that's what made her maddest.

• • •

"So Byrne's the ball-buster who's had you laying off the brew?" Carlyle, having heard the commotion, leaned on the bar and offered Ian a shit-eating grin. "That's amazing."

Beside Carlyle, Sanchez laughed. "She's your baseball wife."

"She's your *wife*?" asked the confused woman, who, until recently, had been sitting on Ian's lap.

"No." But Pauly was important enough to Ian that his gut burned and his head pounded just thinking about how upset she'd been. And the night before a start. He was a total dick. He never would've come here if he'd known she was planning on being here, too.

"A round of shots," Carlyle called out to the bartender. "Because we can." He looked right at Ian, like it was some warped show of independence wrapped in solidarity.

Sure, Ian *could* have a shot. The damage was already done. Pauly wasn't going to forgive him anytime soon, and two ounces of hard liquor might quiet the guilt. But the thought of drinking made him sick.

The bartender lined up the shots. Carlyle did some weird wipe with his finger under his nose, like he was preparing to snort the shit. Sanchez made piercing, hyena-like noises. And Martinez, who'd joined at the mention of shots, bent forward to dip the tip of his tongue into the whiskey.

Only the woman, whose name Ian had somehow missed, despite her talking her way onto his lap, seemed normal as she waited for her drink.

And in his head the same words echoed: *What the hell are you doing here?*

Nobody had chained him up and dragged him here. He'd chosen to come. Insisted on it, really. Blocked Pauly out at the stadium every time she'd tried to get through to him. And why? To fulfill some warped destiny. But he could've chosen differently. He could still choose differently.

Pauly's voice infiltrated his head. *Nobody's stopping you but you.* It was what she'd been trying to tell him all along. Even in the clubhouse before the game, when he was too far into himself to break free.

"On three," Carlyle said.

Sanchez literally panted.

Martinez rubbed his palms together greedily.

"Uno!" Carlyle yelled.

They were a bunch of idiots, shooting pool and shots the night before Game Four in a championship series.

"Two!" Carlyle yelled.

Ian wasn't a benchwarmer anymore. He wasn't riding the pine watching the game go by. He was in the thick of it. Making decisions on the fly. Contributing to the outcome. Tomorrow was as much his big game as it was Pauly's.

"Three!"

"I don't belong here." Ian climbed off the stool.

"Where you going?" Carlyle asked, the hint of a whine in his voice.

"I'm going home," Ian said.

"Dude." Sanchez gave him freaking puppy-dog eyes.

Ian slid the beer and shot across the bar toward him. "You can have mine. I didn't touch either."

Then he walked out of Foley's, not knowing if he'd ever go back.

All he knew right now was he needed to find Pauly.

• • •

Ian didn't know where Pauly was headed, but he hoped she was headed home. That was the first place he intended to look when he drove his truck out of Foley's parking lot, but he didn't get very far.

Across the street from the bar, he saw a large man pacing back and forth in front of the pancake house. If it weren't for the color of the guy's skin, Ian probably wouldn't have taken a second look. But Pauly had been right when she'd said there weren't a lot of black people in Arlington.

Ian swung his truck around at the nearest break in the boulevard, pulling a U-ey at the bank. When he pulled into the pancake house lot, the guy was still having an animated phone conversation. Which was a bonus, because Ian didn't want or need any interference.

Unfortunately, the guy recognized Ian the minute he got out of his truck.

"Yo. How you doin', man?" The words were friendly, but the posture wasn't.

Ian couldn't exactly blame him. Besides, he liked the idea of someone looking out for Pauly—even though she didn't need it.

"I've been better," Ian said. "I'm hoping a quick chat with your sister will fix that."

"Ain't gonna happen." And, yep, the dude puffed out his already intimidating chest.

Ian was no slouch. He squared his shoulders, more to balance out the situation than to scare the guy. "I don't think we've ever been introduced," he said. "I'm Ian Pratt. I catch for Pauly." He extended his hand.

The man looked at it. He cocked his head and made a face, but then he grabbed Ian's hand and squeezed. As hard as a vise. "Devon Byrne."

Ian decided to run with it. "Devon, man, I need to talk to her."

"You said enough in the bar."

"But, I didn't, and that's the problem." He waited a few seconds more, for Devon to concede willingly. When he didn't, Ian tried to sidestep him. "I won't take long."

Devon was big, but he was quick, and he blocked Ian before he had a real shot at the door.

"Dude." Ian raised his hands in surrender. "I'm not a fighter."

"If you say you're a lover, I'm going to throat-punch you."

Ian put a hand to his throat. "Nope. I wasn't going anywhere near that word. Because I'm not … that word … with your sister … if that's what you meant." *Shit.*

Devon crossed his thick arms across his body and glowered. Ian wasn't easily intimidated, but he took a step back.

"That's it," Devon said. "Keep on walking."

Ian stopped. Something clicked. And he exhaled. "I would, but I can't until I know she's okay."

"She will be. She's in there trying to calm down. And I won't risk you upsetting her again. So you better leave before she sees you."

"That's not gonna work. I know Pauly, and she's going to stew on what happened back there until the game tomorrow, and it's going to mess everything up between us." As innocent as he'd meant it, "us" probably wasn't the best word choice under the circumstances. "Because we're friends," Ian added. "Just friends." If it would save his throat and Pauly the aggravation, he would twist the truth.

"You think you know my sister better than me?" Devon didn't wait for an answer. "I know my sister, and she doesn't need a *friend* out on the field. She needs a teammate who takes the game as seriously as she does."

"And that's me," Ian said sincerely. "That's who I am. I don't want her thinking I'm back to being the dick she first met."

Devon shook his head. "Dude, don't you get it? She shouldn't be thinking about you at all. She's less than twenty-four hours away from the biggest game of her life. That's where her focus should be. And if you know what's good for you—what's good for her—you'll get back in that truck and go home and get ready to play."

Ian glanced at the shiny restaurant windows, looking for any sign of Pauly or any sign of what he should do next. Brawling with her brother to get inside didn't seem like the answer. And, *hell*, maybe Devon was right. Maybe the best thing Ian could do was not disturb her focus again. But it didn't feel right to let her fester and think the worst of him.

Ian nodded. "I appreciate you trying to protect her, but I gotta be honest, man. If I get back in my truck, I'm just going to sit there until she comes out. And maybe I'll text her, because she needs to know the truth about what happened back there."

Devon glanced at the building behind him and sighed. "You're not gonna give up, are you?"

A month ago, he sure as hell would've. "Nope."

Devon stepped aside. "The throat-chop threat still stands."

"Got it," Ian said, adding a nervous laugh.

When he entered the restaurant, he saw her sitting at the back booth, her shoulders slumped and her head in her hands, and he hated himself for causing this turmoil.

Her other brother stood as Ian and Devon walked closer. Pauly stayed seated, but she turned, and the minute her eyes met his, her expression hardened.

"Why are you here?" she asked.

"To talk," Ian said.

The brothers faded off into another part of the restaurant, and Ian slid onto the bench across from her.

"It doesn't matter what you say, Ian. I'm not going to forget what I saw back there. I'm not going to go back to thinking there could ever be anything meaningful between us."

He swallowed against an uncomfortable ball of emotion. Seriously. What had he expected to happen? "There *is* something meaningful between us."

"Not anymore. Not beyond the relationship on the field. And that's only for one more game."

"What about next season?"

She shrugged. "Maybe Tuck will be back."

It pierced like a shard of glass through his heart. "Maybe."

He had more to say, but if that was how she really felt, he didn't see the sense of saying it. "So this is it?"

"This is it." She sounded strong and sure.

He nodded. "And it won't affect the way we play tomorrow?"

"You tell me. You're the one who registered three passed balls today." She twisted the glass shard effortlessly.

"Does it mean anything to you that I didn't take a single drink?"

"No. Because it means more that you went there at all. You went there instead of coming to me, when I knew something was bothering you. You shut down. You shut me out. That says it all."

He hung his head. He'd never been so disappointed in himself before, and he couldn't think of a way to make things better. "I know you think I'm just like my father. I thought that, too, but I'm not, Pauly. I'm not."

"Actions speak louder than words," she said flatly.

She was right.

He slid to the end of the bench and stood, pausing briefly at her side. "Then I'm going to prove it to you."

Chapter Fifteen

After falling asleep at his computer in the middle of reading scouting reports and dragging himself to bed in the wee hours of the morning, Ian awoke shortly after noon, surprisingly fresh and ready to roll. He was prepared, and he was a professional. Nothing that had happened before today mattered—at least, not while they were on the field.

He kept those two words—prepared and professional—in his head while he drove to the stadium for batting practice. Five minutes from the turnoff, his phone rang.

Aunt May.

Ian didn't even get in a hello.

"He's having a seizure!" she shrieked. "I think he's dying!"

Her shrill voice went right through Ian, and he yanked the steering wheel hard to the right, pulling off to the side of the road. "He's not dying." He couldn't be dying. "Did you call 9-1-1?"

"Not yet."

"Call them now!" Ian glanced behind him and pulled the truck back onto the empty road, heading in the opposite direction. "I'm on my way."

It took him ten minutes to drive the twenty minutes back to his father's place. When he got there, Aunt May was kneeling on the floor with Ray's head resting on her legs.

"It passed," she said, but by the looks of her white face and disheveled hair, it hadn't passed soon enough.

Ian squatted beside his father, whose eyes were closed and mouth was open. His breath rattled somewhere in the back of his throat, and sweat glistened on his brow.

"Dad." Ian pressed a hand to the old guy's stubbly cheek, and something just broke inside of him. "*Jesus*, what have you done to yourself?"

May sniffled above him. "It shook him right out of his chair. I called 9-1-1 like you told me to."

Ian didn't even want to think about how this might've played out if his aunt hadn't been here. "Thank you." He squeezed her hand and went to the window, where faint strains of sirens filtered through the glass. "I hear them. Hang on, Dad."

Ten minutes later, Ray was strapped to a gurney and wheeled into the ambulance, and Ian was trying to decide his next step. Your actions wouldn't prove anything if you weren't there, and this was the worst possible game for him to miss. People were depending on him. Pauly was depending on him. But what about his dad and May?

"I'll follow behind you," May said to the young paramedic, and then she pointed at Ian. "Thank you for coming, but you need to go. You're going to be late."

Ian shook his head. "I'm already late." Any minute now his phone would light up.

May backed toward her car. "You can't help him now. Leave it to the professionals. Help yourself. Don't mess this up. Ray said it was a big game."

Those words, they echoed in his ears. "He told you that."

She nodded as she opened her car door. "That's why he got out of bed this morning. He was planning on going. We both were. And trust me, when that man wakes up, he's going to want to know what happened at the game."

That was all she needed to say. Ian raced to this truck and hauled ass to the stadium, arriving forty-five minutes past report time, but still two and a half hours before the first pitch. Now, if he could just get focused.

"Pratt!"

He stopped several feet from the locker-room door and faced an angry-looking Coach Slater.

"Skip, my dad. We had to call 9-1-1. I'm sorry."

"He okay?"

Ian nodded. "He had a seizure. He'll be fine."

"Good. Your damn phone broken?"

"No, sir."

"Then you should've called me."

"Yes, sir. I wasn't exactly thinking straight."

Wrong answer. Coach's face wrinkled. "And you're thinking straight now?"

"Yes, sir."

Coach tilted his head and seemed to be weighing something. "Pratt, there's something you should know. Mason is back."

Ian's blood ran cold. "I thought it was a lifetime suspension."

"He appealed, and he proved a false positive."

The ground felt shaky, which made Ian think about his dad. And then, rapid-fire, his brain switched gears to Pauly. Was she with Tuck now, warming up for the game? "Am I—"

"I don't know," Coach said. "I have a lot to chew on. You showing up late with some heavy stuff on your mind included."

"But I can play, Skip. I *want* to play."

"That's what Mason said, too. And he has the more accurate arm when it comes to pickoffs. He's also logged a helluva lot more games with Byrne on the mound."

"But she doesn't like last-minute changes. We're in sync now."

"I know. Something else to chew on, and it's a mouthful for a championship series, lemme tell ya." Coach hitched his pants a little higher on his belly. "I won't make this call without talking to Byrne, so get dressed and get warmed up. You'll have my decision by game time."

Ian watched Coach Slater return to his office, a heavy dose of disappointment rooting him in place. After what had happened between Ian and Pauly yesterday, Tuck Mason had to be looking like a damn good alternative. Especially after Ian had shown up late to this game. But he wasn't giving up yet. Pauly deserved to know why he was late, and Ian deserved a chance to set the record straight.

• • •

Physically, Pauly felt good. Warm and loose. She'd stretched, thrown, and shagged some flies for the guys taking batting practice. Now, she was back in her own little corner of the stadium, sitting in a folding chair, staring at the wall, trying to get centered when what she really wanted to do was text Pratt and find out where he was. Tell him Mason was here. Tell him she was one thought away from losing it—just to hear him say she was strong and ready. And that pissed her off, because even though she didn't *need* anybody, she still wanted him.

The door opened behind her, and she saw Ian dressed in his street clothes, hard lines across his face. All the anger she'd felt toward him took a backseat to a fresh surge of concern.

"What happened?" she asked, coming to her feet.

He shook his head but said, "My dad had a seizure. My aunt had to call 9-1-1."

"Is he okay now?"

"I think so. He's in good hands. Pauly—"

"Mason's back."

"I know. Skip stopped me in the hall. He's going to be headed this way to you … to talk about which one of us gets the start. And listen, as much as I want to play in this game, as much as I've come to believe I deserve to play in this game, standing here right now, looking at you, all I can think about is giving you whatever *you* need to win. What do you need? If it's Tuck Mason behind the plate, then so be it. I'll walk down to Skip's office and tell him to sit me. But before you answer that, you gotta hear me out." He reached for her hand, and she let him wrap it in his. "I've been thinking a lot, trying to decide why I even put myself in that position yesterday, and all I can come up with is that I'm scared."

"Of what?" she whispered.

"I used to think it was a fear of getting dragged down, but now I think it's a fear of not being able to get back up. Like my mom." His voice cracked, and her heart broke. "I worry about screwing up. About letting you down. Letting myself down. It's a lot easier to wake up every morning and face another day when you have nothing to lose. But that's not how I want to live. Not anymore."

His crisp, clear eyes said it all. He cared about her, maybe even as much as she cared about him, but she couldn't go down this road two hours before a game.

"Ian, you asked me what I need to win, and it's me." She nodded confidently. "Just me. But don't take that the wrong way. It's just that I know deep down it doesn't matter who's behind the plate. I'm the one on the mound. I'm the one who's throwing. And I know exactly what I'm capable of. So whatever Skip decides will be fine with me. But"—she took a step closer, wanting him to know she cared about him, too—"no matter where you are, in my head, I'll be throwing to you."

His expression twisted as he pressed her palm to his lips for a kiss. Her knees weakened, and her breathing hitched.

"Pauly, you're—"

Someone knocked on the door, which was ajar, and Ian dropped her hand.

Coach Slater stuck his head around the jamb. He didn't make eye contact with them, like he was worried about what he might see, and his voice was gruff when he said, "Private conversations usually happen behind *closed* doors."

He'd heard everything. Surprisingly, Pauly was too hopped up on adrenaline and emotion to care.

"But I'm glad that one didn't," he added. Then, he looked at Ian. "You got the start, Pratt, so you better get your ass dressed and out there before I regret it."

"Yes, sir." Ian hugged the man, and with a smile for Pauly, he left.

"That bit about you only needing yourself?" Coach asked, now that they were alone. "Good stuff. Just remember you have seven more guys behind you on that field, and it's okay to lean on them when you need to. Perfect games are rare."

"I know."

But that didn't mean she couldn't aim for one.

• • •

The first six innings flew by in a rush of adrenaline and the roar of the crowd. Six innings. Nine batters. Thirty pitches. No men on base. It was insane. But, somehow, Pauly maintained her cool. Nobody mentioned the obvious in the dugout—that, so far, she was pitching a perfect game. And Pauly, though aware of it, too, didn't give it more than a passing thought. She didn't have to be perfect to win a championship.

Coach gave her the nod to head back out for the seventh inning, and she stood on the mound, facing home plate. Breathing in. Breathing out. Ready to face her tenth batter of the day. Alvin Murdock. His strength was that he could turn on an inside pitch and drive it. His weakness was that he liked to reach out to pull a ball. Last time she'd faced him, in the regular season, she'd baited him with a fastball straight down the pipe, followed by two backdoor sliders that struck him out swinging. But she didn't want to be predictable. *Throw something he isn't expecting.* Based on their history, that would be a curveball.

Ian flashed two fingers between his legs, calling for a curve, and she hid a small smile behind her glove as she confirmed the pitch.

The windup. The pitch. Pauly watched the ball break across the plate and end up outside.

"Steee-rike!" wailed the home-plate ump.

Pauly reset. Murdock had been so far off the ball, she wanted to try that pitch again.

Ian signaled for another curveball.

This time, Murdock reached out and got a piece of it, knocking it foul, giving her heart a little jolt. *No more curveballs.*

Since the slider was just a faster, harder curve with less downward action, she started to doubt that pitch, too. And just like that, momentum shifted. Murdock walked, and Pauly blew her perfect game.

Ian lifted his mask as he jogged toward the mound. "I thought we had him."

"Me, too." Her limbs hung heavy with disappointment.

"I don't want to jinx anything, but it's still a no-hitter. Right?"

Her gaze skirted Ian's head to the spot behind the plate where scouts sat with clipboards and stopwatches. A no-hitter to win a championship would be pretty beast.

And just like that, momentum shifted again. Pauly followed Murdock with two strikeouts to end her seventh inning.

"Skip," she said in the dugout, when he approached. "I'm going back out for the eighth."

He grinned. "If you think I'd pull you now, you're crazy."

The eighth flashed by. Three batters. Nine pitches. No men on base.

She glanced at the scoreboard. 2-0, Aces. Then she glanced at the scouts again. She wondered if they knew she was pitching for her life.

Unfortunately, that heavy thought stuck with her when she took the field in the ninth. The first hitter connected with a meatball and lined out to second. No real harm. The second batter fought hard, and it took eight nail-biting pitches to retire him. By now, Pauly was fatigued, so it was no surprise when she walked the third batter after almost mowing him down with an errant pitch.

Coach McKellar came out to give her a boost. "Do you have more gas in that tank?"

"Yes, sir," she said. "Enough to finish this game."

"Then wipe the slate clean, and start over with this next batter. He's gonna be your last, Ace. I can feel it."

She could feel it too. Even so, she worked the count full.

Ian called time, and she stepped off the mound to meet him. She welcomed the reset.

"Ignore the base runner," he said. "Whaddya know about this batter?"

She rattled off a list. "Why? What do you know?"

Ian grinned behind his mitt—she could tell by the wrinkled skin around his eyes. His bell had gone off. "He set up in the back of the box last time, but now, his feet are closer to you. He's looking to bunt, or he wants a jump on your curve before it has time to break. You're already in his head."

She nodded.

"Let's fuck with him," Ian said, and by the lift of his brow she knew he was thinking knuckleball.

It was risky. She hadn't thrown one today. If she was off, it could advance the runner and blow the no-hitter. But if she was on, it could end the game.

"Trust me," Ian said. "Trust yourself."

"I do."

She climbed the mound again. Exhaled. Visualized the perfect pitch. She set her body, adjusted her fingers, and the strangest calm came over her. *Trust yourself.* She really did. Without a doubt. She was going to be okay no matter what happened here, no matter where she ended up after baseball. But that wasn't now. And it didn't have to be next season either. If she had to live with a host family and bus to the stadium and live on ramen noodles like the other guys, she could stand on her own two feet. Which meant Holymount and coaching could wait. Because baseball couldn't. Neither could the way she felt about Ian Pratt. She loved him. Even though it complicated everything.

Between his legs, Ian wiggled fingers that didn't mean a damn thing, because they'd already determined their pitch. The air stilled. The crowd silenced. And Pauly could've sworn she literally heard the ball sailing toward the batter. She tracked its erratic path all the way in, barely breathing.

A swing. A miss. An eruption from the crowd.

The Aces were champions.

Chapter Sixteen

After the trophy presentation, Ian huddled in the only halfway-quiet corner he could find in the clubhouse, where he strained to listen to Aunt May's update on his dad while he dodged sprays of champagne.

"They said the increased dosage will help."

"How is he now?" Ian asked, shoving a finger deeper into his ear to make sure he caught every word.

"Sleeping, but when he wakes up, I'll have him call you."

"Don't worry about it. I'll be there soon. When he wakes up, I want to tell him his son is a champion." It felt surreal. From that perfect knuckleball to the trophy presentation at home plate to the chaos going on around him. The Arlington Aces had won their first Independence League championship, and Ian had been a major contributor. But Pauly deserved the loudest accolades. She'd pitched the first no-hitter in organization history, and according to Skip, it was also the only no-hitter in the Independence League this season.

They were definitely going to have some serious fun celebrating that.

Ian ended his call and rejoined his team. Despite sheets of plastic hanging from the ceiling and covering furniture and carpets, champagne managed to seep into everything, including down his back and into his cleats. He had to laugh, though, because not a drop had made it into his mouth, and he was happy to keep it that way.

"Attention, please!" Coach Slater stood at the front of the room with the rest of the staff. His hands were raised in authority, and his voice reinforced the sentiment, but it was hard to take a guy wearing a batting helmet rigged with pharmaceutical tubing and two opened cans of beer seriously. "Quiet down. Someone special would like to say a few words."

Between the bodies, Ian glimpsed the team owner, Rachel Reed, dressed in her usual—sky-high heels and an "Aces blue" suit. She was easy on the eyes but hard on the balls, and apparently, that was exactly what this team needed. Sam Sutter was one lucky bastard. But not as lucky as Ian. After all, Ian was the guy who got to be on the receiving end of Pauly Byrne's pitches.

He smiled amid memories of the conversation Coach Slater had thankfully overheard. He owed her everything for keeping him in that game. She stood near the front of the crowd now, drinking champagne straight from the bottle. Stringy, wet curls spilled down her back, covering the last name on her jersey. And he wanted her, like he'd never wanted anything else.

But before Ian could get anywhere near her, he saw someone else. Rachel Reed's father, John, the original owner of the team, was dressed in a business suit he couldn't quite fill out. He sat at the front of the room in a wheelchair, wearing an Aces cap and a mostly blank expression on his face. Four years ago, the man had been diagnosed with Alzheimer's, and the disease had finally gotten the best of him.

Rachel rolled her father into the middle of the room, and the clubhouse went still.

"Dad," she said, kneeling beside him. "Do you know where we are?"

The frail man looked around but didn't say a word.

"We're at Federal Field in the clubhouse," she said. "You own a baseball team. Remember?"

Slowly, the man nodded, and then he touched the brim of his cap with one shaky hand.

"Remember how you used to come in here and tell everyone we were going to win a championship?" Rachel continued, her voice wavering. "Well, we did it, Dad. We won."

Normally, the clubhouse would've exploded on a proclamation like that, but nobody moved. It was all Ian could do to blink.

Mr. Reed's gaze shifted from his daughter to the crowd of coaches and ballplayers.

"What do you think about that, Dad?"

With what looked like every ounce of energy the man had left, he raised his hand and gave the room a thumbs-up, followed by a smile.

That did it. The room erupted. A few errant streams of champagne shot toward the ceiling and tumbled down again while even more champagne flew around the room and players' families trickled in. The private meeting was over, which was Ian's cue to head to the hospital. But first, he needed to talk to Pauly.

"Hey," he said, coming up behind her, setting his hand in the crook of her waist.

"Hey." She turned and smiled with lips glistening wet from champagne.

He had the raging urge to kiss her, but he kept it in check, leaning in until his mouth was against her ear, telling himself it was the only way she could hear him. But that was bullshit. Ever since she'd looked at him with those stormy gray eyes and told him no matter where he was she'd be pitching to him, he wanted to be as close to her as possible for as long as she would have him.

"Guess we finally proved you can go nine innings," he said.

She threw back her head and laughed.

The unbridled joy made it harder to leave, but … "I need to go see my dad."

She nodded and slipped a warm, soft hand to his elbow. He wasn't the kind of man who shuddered, but, *Jesus*, she laid him out.

"Do you want me to come with you?" she asked.

"No. I don't want you to miss the celebration." *Screw it.* He pulled her closer, mentally giving double fingers to anyone who might care. "But I do want to see you later." He brushed a soft kiss over her champagne-coated lips.

Her fingers drifted higher beneath his sleeves as she leaned into him. "I need to talk to you, too."

That wasn't exactly what he had in mind, and the response unsettled him. But the longer they stood there like that—connected—the more he just didn't care. No matter what she had to say, he doubted there would be much talking anyway.

• • •

Pauly was holding a half-full bottle of champagne in one hand and her phone set to video mode in the other when Rachel Reed tugged on her elbow.

"Can I steal you for a second?" Rachel glanced at the green bottle with the bright orange label. "And bring the champagne."

Pauly didn't ask questions. She floated along behind Rachel, aided by too many bubbles in her brain.

"We'll go up to my office, where it's quiet," Rachel said the minute the clubhouse door closed behind them.

Office sounded official, but Rachel wanted champagne. Pauly shrugged and took another drink. Maybe she was going to get a gift. One woman to another. That had to be it.

"Thanks for taking a chance on me," Pauly said, feeling sentimental.

Rachel stopped outside the elevator and turned sharp eyes on Pauly. "*Please.* It was never a chance. It was a no-brainer."

Pauly liked the way this woman thought. She smiled and followed Rachel into the elevator. "Congratulations on the championship."

Rachel's face brightened, and the usual lines of intense concentration faded away. "Thank you. It's unreal. This entire journey." She kicked off her heels and relaxed against the elevator wall. "Some days everything just falls into place." She reached for the champagne bottle and took a long drink.

Pauly leaned against the opposite wall and laughed. She was drinking champagne with the team owner after throwing a no-hitter to win a championship. Unreal? How about unbelievable?

Rachel passed the bottle back as the elevator chimed and the doors slid open. "You're going to need that," she said with a sly smile.

Well, yeah, but … "There's a lot more downstairs."

Rachel walked into the reception area of the administration level that overlooked the field, which was still glowing with post-game activity. Pauly had only been up here a few times before, so the wonder if it all had never worn off. Gleaming wood, custom carpets sporting the Aces caricature logo. Hard to believe something like this existed in a place like Arlington.

"This way," Rachel said, and she ducked into an office at the end of the hall.

For some reason, Pauly's pulse took off in a dead sprint the minute she crossed the threshold into the room. *Too much champagne.* She set the bottle on the huge glass desk in front of her and faced Rachel, who'd closed the door.

"You can sit," Rachel said.

"I'll stand." This didn't feel like a simple post-game celebration anymore.

"Okay." Rachel rounded her desk, tossed her heels onto the seat of a cushy-looking leather chair, and exhaled. "Pauly Byrne, in case you didn't notice, there were scouts at the game."

Her heart jackhammered against her ribs. "Oh, I noticed," she said, mentally crossing her fingers that one of them had approached Rachel about buying Pauly's contract. To do it all in the same game would be fast, but not unheard of, and since no agents or managers were allowed in the Independence League, it would also be done on the sly. It was possible. Definitely possible.

"The scouts were here to see you," Rachel said. "They're still here, and after this little meeting, they're going to come in and congratulate you, because it's my honor to inform you that your contract has been purchased by the Cleveland Indians."

Pauly sat. On the floor. Because the damn chair was too far away. "What?" she croaked, her heart beating so violently it interfered with her breathing. "I mean, I hoped. I worked. I thought maybe something would come from today, but—"

"It's actually been in process for weeks, and it became official yesterday. Which makes you the first woman to be signed by a major-league baseball team. Ever."

Tears streamed down Pauly's cheeks, and her hands shook. "Is this really happening?"

"Yes, it is." Rachel's voice seemed strained, and her face grew splotchy. "Congratulations. You deserve it."

"Holy shit!" Pauly threw her head back and screamed with joy, a scream that turned into hysterical laughter. And then she pushed off the floor, grabbed the champagne bottle, guzzled a mouthful, and ended up in a chair. "I never suspected anything."

Rachel finally sat, too. "I thought about telling you sooner, but I knew you wouldn't have any objections to the sale of your contract. Then I thought telling you might impact the way you approached these last few games, and I didn't want to mess up the momentum. So, ultimately, I decided to sit on it. Cleveland wants the information embargoed until you're in town for a press conference anyway. That'll take place the day after tomorrow. Eddie Ranch and Paul Nixon will tell you more when you meet with them. And don't worry. They know you've been celebrating, and they won't keep you long. They just want to congratulate you in person."

God, her head was spinning. "So it's a secret?"

"A big one. Your whole world's going to change with this announcement, Pauly. I don't know where in their farm system you'll end up playing, but wherever it is, you're going to be a big deal. This has *never* happened before."

"Oh. My. God." She rubbed a hand over her face and tried to process it. *Really* process it, so it settled into her toes and grounded her in a way that would set her up for success.

Tonight, she was a champion. In two days, she would be starting from the bottom all over again. Even if she landed in short season Single-A, she was committed to making the climb. Best of all, no matter where Cleveland put her, she still got to wake up every day and play baseball.

"Oh my God," she said again. "My dad is gonna freak!" All these years. All this work. All the pep talks. "I can tell him, right?"

Rachel nodded. "Your immediate family, but they're held to the embargo as well, so not a word." She zipped her fingers across her lips.

"What about the team?" Pauly asked, when really, she only wanted to tell Ian.

"We'll figure something out, but not tonight, okay? Everybody's been drinking, and the clubhouse is filled with other people. Too many variables."

Pauly nodded. "Okay. Thank you," she said, pressing her hands together in prayer formation. "For everything."

Rachel rounded the desk and surprised Pauly with a hug. "Thank *you*. Now go out there and make us even prouder."

•••

After a brief meeting with the scouts, who would see her again tomorrow morning, Pauly told her family to meet her in the relative privacy of the stadium rotunda. The four of them were dressed head-to-toe in Aces gear. Her mother in a custom, bedaz-zled Byrne jersey. Her father in his lucky quarter-zip sweater. And her brothers in T-shirts and ball caps. They bum-rushed her the minute the elevator doors opened.

Screams. Hollers. She couldn't make out too many words. She fell into their arms, laughing, and the whole time, she was thinking, *You have* no *idea*.

When she couldn't hold it in any longer, she raised her head above her mother's shoulder and said, "You guys!" But nobody heard her over the fuss.

"Best game you've ever pitched," her father said.

"So proud of you," her mother added.

Meanwhile, her brothers launched into an off-key rendition of "We Are the Champions."

"Guys!" Pauly pulled out of the group hug and raised her hands above her head. "I gotta tell you something."

They stared at her, stepped back, and grew eerily quiet.

She hadn't considered it before, but she probably looked crazed. Hair wet, uniform soiled, so much adrenaline pumping through her veins she couldn't stand still. But who cared? After the amazing day she'd had, she was entitled to it.

"Guys." She grinned, lowered her voice, and tried to contain her excitement in case someone else was milling around. "My contract has been purchased by the Cleveland Indians." By the time she'd gotten to "Indians," she was shouting.

Her family was shouting, too.

They pulled her into another aggressive hug, bouncing her up and down. Squealing. Laughing. Crying.

She looked up from the center of the circle and saw her father's watery eyes.

"See, Dad?" she said. "No more worries." She grabbed his hand and squeezed. "I had everything under control the whole time."

He smiled, even as he sniffed back the emotion.

As the reality of the situation sunk in, they all calmed down, and the questions appeared.

"When do you leave?" her father asked.

"Day after tomorrow."

"Where will you end up?" Devon asked.

"In the majors," she said with confidence.

"No shit," Trey said, punching her playfully in the arm. "But where are you going to start out?"

"I don't know."

"I hope it's not too far away." Her mother frowned.

"We'll manage," her father said, taking her mother's hand. "And as long as I'm unemployed, I have a more flexible schedule, so we can travel." He sounded happy about the job loss for the first time.

"Maybe you won't have to work at all, Dad," Pauly said. "Either one of you." She looked at her mother, too. "I can get an agent now. I can start making real money off my brand." The possibilities were endless. She glanced skyward, so grateful, before she added, "It's my turn to support you."

"One step at a time, P." Her father slung an arm affectionately around her shoulders and pulled her in. "One step at a time."

Maybe, but tonight she felt like she'd bypassed simple steps, and from here on out, she'd be soaring. Next stop: Ian.

They needed to figure out what all of this meant for them.

Chapter Seventeen

Ian found Pauly sitting on the steps outside his townhouse. It wasn't a surprise, because she'd texted him while he was at the hospital to tell him she was on her way.

"I told you the code," he said. "Why didn't you go in?"

"Nice night," she said thoughtfully. "The stars remind me of camp."

He looked at the bursts of light in the pitch-black sky and thought about the hunting camp. He used to think if he lost that place, he'd lose himself, too. Now, he wasn't so sure. He was just starting to understand who Ian Pratt was and what he was capable of. Thanks to Pauly Byrne.

She was still looking up, bare arms wrapped around her knees, holding them close to her chest. She did something to him just by breathing.

"You look cold," he said.

She rested her chin on her knee and shook her head. "I can't really feel anything."

He was going to change that.

"How's your dad?" she asked.

"Being a pain in the ass, which means he's fine. He should be released tomorrow."

"That's good."

"I don't know about that. The man's a hurricane. I don't know how my aunt puts up with him. He treats her like—"

"Ian?"

He stopped talking. Her eyes widened. She looked like she wanted to jump out of her skin. "Yeah?"

"The Indians bought my contract."

The words knocked the wind right out of him. He leaned forward and dropped to the step beside her. "No shit?"

"No shit."

"Wow." So this was it? She was leaving. It wasn't some hypothetical decision she may or may not have to make later this fall or after next season. He was going to find out firsthand if he had the strength to let her go without ending up like his father.

"I know."

"This is … great!" It was. He had no business making it about him.

He slung an arm around her shoulder and pulled her in for a hug. She was leaving. She'd always been leaving. Pauly Byrne was bigger than this place.

"MLB," he said as he pressed his lips against her temple. "Damn."

"Is that a happy damn or a sad damn?" she asked, pulling back to look at him.

Her eyes sparkled silver in the moonlight, and they flickered over his face like they could read his mind.

He tucked a curl behind her ear and smoothed his thumb along her jawline. "Can it be both?"

"Yep. As long as happy's in there somewhere, because that's how I'm feeling, too." She smiled briefly. "I'm a little torn."

She dropped her head to his shoulder and settled in, one hand on his thigh, the other around his waist.

He tightened his grip on her. "When do you leave?"

"Day after tomorrow."

"Damn," he said again, resting his cheek against her head. "And that wasn't a happy one."

"I know. It seems fast."

"But it's not. Nobody sticks around after their contract has been sold."

She nodded. "I should thank you."

If she wanted to thank him the way she had in the stadium parking lot against the bed of his truck, he'd be more than fine with that. Anything to make him stop feeling like he was losing her.

"Rachel said this has been in the works for weeks," she continued. "Which means I could've blown it without knowing it if you hadn't kept my head in some of those games."

He smoothed his hand up and down her arm. "You're giving me too much credit."

"I don't think so. It's a team effort, you know?"

He chuckled. "Then why didn't the Indians pick up the whole team?"

She was quiet for a few beats, and then she lifted her head to look at him. "Ian, what happens now?"

He got the feeling deep in his gut she was asking about what happened to them—after she left. But there was no way he wanted to think about that, not when she was looking up at him with those shiny eyes and that kissable mouth.

"I'm going to take you to bed," he said.

"I was hoping you would say that."

Ian had run this scenario a million times in his head, and never once did it involve a bed. Up against a wall, a door, hell, even in the locker room. But now that it was here—along with this news he could barely fathom—the bed made sense. He wanted to take it slow and easy, since it looked like they only had tonight.

He took her hand and pulled her to stand.

"I'm nervous," she said.

"About this?"

She shook her head, and a smile tipped up her lips. "No. I'm nervous about Cleveland."

"You wouldn't be human if you weren't nervous about Cleveland. It snows like a mother up there."

She laughed, and it resonated in his chest. "Thank you." As her laughter faded, more meaning littered her face, and the intensity rattled him. "For believing in me."

"Ditto." The word sounded funny exiting his tight throat, so he kissed her. He slid his hand to her neck and slipped his tongue into her mouth, and he held her there, transferring the heaviness deep inside of him into the kiss. And when he'd lightened up and softened in all but one place, he pulled back and led her into the condo.

"Do you have condoms?" she asked as they climbed the stairs.

"Yes."

"Good. Because I don't, which is odd for a woman who always likes to be prepared, don't you think?"

He laughed as he pulled her into his bedroom and into his arms. "Pauly, nothing about you is odd. You're perfect. I've wanted you from the moment I saw you."

"No, you didn't."

"It's true. Seeing those tight polyester pants hugging this great ass. Game after game." He smoothed his hands over her curves and held her against his erection, loving the way her breath hitched in the dark. "Four fucking seasons of trying to pretend I didn't notice that. I'm surprised it didn't kill me."

"Is that supposed to make me feel bad for you?" She slipped a hand between them and pressed it along the length of his zipper.

"No." His voice was low and gravelly. "It's just a warning."

"Please." She laughed and nipped at the underside of his chin. "Your four seasons of torment are nothing compared to two years without an orgasm."

"Two years? Not even—"

"Those don't count," she said, cutting him off with her words and then her mouth.

Hot mental images of her pleasuring herself coupled with the physical sensation of her driving into his mouth eradicated any hopes he'd had of taking it slow and easy.

She shoved his shirt over his abs, and he ripped it over his head. Hers sailed to the floor next. They were a flurry of mouths and hands and heavy breathing when they crashed to the mattress behind him.

Her bare breasts smacked against his chest. Somewhere along the line she'd managed to rid herself of her bra, too. Points for enthusiasm. But one of these days, he wanted to undress her slowly and get another good long look at every inch of her body. And just like that, the miserable time constraint was back, messing with his head, splintering his heart. He didn't want this to be it. He didn't want her to go.

Shit.

He scrambled off the bed and into an upright position just so he could breathe.

"Ian?"

With his blackout drapes still pulled from the night before, the room was dark, so dark he couldn't make out the details of her face, which meant she couldn't possibly know what he looked like in this moment that was tearing him apart. "Right here, babe," he said, as smooth as he could muster. "It's easier to lose the pants like this."

In a burst of shadowy movement, she was at the side of his bed, her hands on his stomach. She unbuttoned and unzipped him, while he took slow, deep breaths, willing himself to take this moment for what it was worth. Pure pleasure.

When she freed him and held him, he growled in appreciation. Then, she kissed his stomach and slid her hand up and down his shaft. Everything he'd been thinking moments ago evaporated in the heat of his desire.

A few more strokes, and he pulled her to her feet. "Christ," he said. "You're gonna finish me before we get started."

She laughed, her lips against his neck. "So you're a one-trick pony?"

He slid a hand between her legs and smiled against her ear, loving the way her breathy whimper hardened him even more. "I'm going to show you all my tricks tonight."

And the pain in his chest deepened.

He settled her back on the bed, keeping a steady rhythm with his fingers between her legs. He kissed her breasts, licked her nipples, and tried like hell to stop thinking and start acting like any normal man who was about to get laid—like the man he used to be. But he couldn't.

When he dragged his mouth down her stomach straight to the heat between her thighs, she moaned his name. And all he could think was this would be the last time he'd ever hear it … unless he could make it so damn good she would always come back to him.

• • •

Pauly came apart against Ian's mouth. The orgasm rang in her ears and buzzed in her blood all the way down to her toes, which curled into his sheets.

"Damn," she breathed, her mouth open. "That's way better than doing it myself."

Ian laughed in between kisses to her stomach. "My services are mobile, you know." The kisses stopped, and she realized it wasn't just an erotic joke made in the literal heat of the moment. He was offering to come wherever she was and do *that* whenever she needed. Talk about a no-brainer. But, what would that make them? What were they now? And whatever it was, was it strong enough to last through this crazy transition with miles and miles between them?

"Ian ..."

His fingers returned to the still pulsing place between her legs. His mouth found her breasts. Deep desire built again, and she shoved her fingers into his hair. *Screw it.* They could talk later—if she had any brain cells left to rub together.

He brought her to orgasm again with just his fingers. And after pulling a condom from a bedside drawer, he knelt between her thighs, running his hands along the length of her body, making her beg with his name.

"Now," she moaned.

"Always," he said, as he buried himself inside of her.

She couldn't think clearly enough to analyze his choice of word. She just hung on to him for dear life and lost herself in the rhythm, coming apart again when he lifted her thigh higher on his hip. She threw her arms around his neck, and he deepened the thrusts, following her over the edge a minute later.

"Stay with me," he whispered roughly against her neck, and *thank God*, he followed that with, "tonight."

He must've rocked her senseless, because she nodded against his heaving chest.

A few minutes later, she nestled her back against his front, way too comfortable in his strong arms.

"I meant what I said." He brushed his lips along her shoulder. "I don't want this to be the end. We're good together."

She forced a laugh. "Ian, I'm not holding you to any of this. It's pillow talk."

"I don't care what you call it. I mean it."

"I believe you *think* you mean it, but you don't do relationships. Remember?"

"That was before you."

Her heart pinched. Somewhere in her mind lived the image of a man who would be strong enough to lean on while she went after this big-league dream. But she didn't want to be Ian's guinea pig, either. She wasn't sure he was capable of making the kind of commitment she needed—not this soon anyway. Tyler couldn't do it after two years of dating. *Two years*, and he still walked away.

"Let's not get too serious," she said softly.

"Man." Ian chuckled in her ear. "Talk about a role reversal."

She closed her eyes at the hint of sadness in his voice. Several silent seconds passed as she warred with her emotions. All she wanted was to backtrack to feeling good instead of feeling confused.

"Did you really show me *all* your tricks?" she asked, shifting her hand beneath the sheets and sliding it up his rock-hard hip. "Because now that we're lying here, I'm wondering if that was all you got."

His hand covered her breast, and his lips pulled on her ear. "Now who's the one with the tricks?"

She wiggled her ass, feeling him harden. "Are they working?"

"Absolutely."

After Ian made love to her again, Pauly fell asleep, surrounded by his arms and his steady breathing. When she woke, he made her breakfast, teased her about packing more than protein bars to take to Cleveland, then kissed her soundly at his front door before she headed home to shower, change, and meet with the scouts again.

"Will I see you tonight?" he asked, still holding her close. "Or is that too *serious*?"

She smiled against his shoulder even as her stomach tied in knots. "Come over to my place later."

Today was going to be a whirlwind. Saying goodbye to her family and teammates. Saying hello to her future. She just wished she knew where that left Ian.

Chapter Eighteen

Last night had been intense. First the championship. Then Pauly's big-league news. Then the sex. And how had Ian tried to top it all? By offering to service her in Cleveland—or wherever she landed—which was exactly what she would've expected from a good-time guy who wanted no strings.

Idiot. Pauly Byrne was too smart for that. If he wanted at shot at her long-term, he was going to have to step up his game. Too bad he wasn't sure what that meant exactly.

At least he had the rest of the day to figure it out.

Before he got too wrapped up in the situation, Ian went to see his dad.

Newly released, but still wearing a hospital bracelet, Ray sat in his recliner with a view of the overgrown backyard outside the window. A folded quilt lay over his legs, which were propped on the footrest. He looked even older but better somehow.

Aunt May blew into the room with a glass of water and a handful of pills. "Raymond, take these, and I'll quit riding your ass."

Ray rolled his eyes, but he listened. When Aunt May headed back to the kitchen, the man leveled Ian with one look. "We need to talk."

"About what?"

"About my situation."

"Which situation?"

"Don't be a smart-ass."

"I'm not. You got a lot going on, Dad. This house. The camp. Your recovery."

"When I say situation, I mean all of it." He whirled his bony hand in the air.

"What's the deal?"

"The deal is, I'm filing chapter 13. May's been talking to one of those lawyers you found, and we've worked out payment plans with my creditors."

"That's good, Dad." Ian had always known it was going to take somebody else to do the heavy lifting. Ray just wasn't the kind of guy to help himself. That right there was the biggest difference between them.

"You can keep your bonus money."

Ian blinked. Under the circumstances, he wouldn't take the half Pauly had promised him, even though he'd won it fair and square, but he didn't mind parting with his half. "I don't need it. I'm back to landscaping full-time next week. Take it, and get a head start on those payments."

Ray shook his head. "I don't want your handout. I want to do this on my own. So it sticks. Take that money and spend it on something that makes you happy."

"She's leaving tomorrow," Ian said soberly.

"You talkin' about your girl?"

Ian nodded. "She's headed to the minors." Pride mixed with misery. Maybe he would buy her something, something to remember him by.

"If you ask me, it's strange to see a woman playing baseball."

"I didn't ask you."

Ray shrugged. "You gonna be in a sour mood for the rest of your life now?"

"I don't know. Maybe."

"Then go with her." Ray said it like it was the most sensible thing in the world.

Ian laughed. "I can't just follow her wherever she goes. That's stalking."

"You can if she feels the same way about you."

Last night, when she'd come apart in his arms, it sure as hell had felt like she did. But that didn't mean she would want him hanging around.

"If I could get the hell out of this chair and go somewhere with someone who made me happy …" Ray's eyes glassed over. "You bet your ass I would. I should've done it years ago, when your mother wanted to. I think she'd still be alive if I'd agreed."

"Mom wanted to leave Arlington?"

Ray nodded. "Before you were born. Her four years were up, and she came home saying she wanted to move to Jamaica and leave the world behind. I thought it was just something she was saying because the military had been so hard on her. I never took her seriously. And then she reenlisted. And then you were born. And …" He roughed a hand over his mouth, and Ian looked away.

It was hard to remember his father hadn't always been a broken man in a worn-out recliner. Ray Pratt had had hopes and dreams. Barbie Pratt had had them, too. Maybe there came a point in every life where you either kept on dreaming, or you gave up and let go. Maybe that had more to do with how you ended up than your circumstances or genetics.

"How serious are you about this girl?" Ray asked.

Ian cleared the emotion from his throat. "Serious enough that I can't imagine spending a day without her."

"Then tell her that."

"I tried. She doesn't believe me. I don't exactly have the best relationship track record."

"Then show her."

Ian had tried that, too. Last night in bed. All that had gotten him was one hell of a role reversal. *Let's not get too serious.*

"And you gotta show her with more than your dick," Ray said, earning a reprimand from Aunt May in the kitchen. "What? It's true. He's been running around with just about anything that breathes. You don't think his girl doesn't know that? Women want the C-word."

"Ray!" Aunt May warned over the sound of running water.

Ian chuckled. "He means commitment, Aunt May. It's all good."

"See? You know." Ray nodded, real proud of himself. "You gotta show her you're capable of *that* if you want to get anywhere."

God. Ian's head was spinning. At this point, even telling her he loved her might not be enough. In fact, he couldn't think of a way to show his level of commitment other than asking her to marry him. But that was batshit crazy. *Wasn't it?*

He sat there with the idea rolling around in his head. Baseball didn't have an equivalent to football's Hail Mary pass, but if it did, asking Pauly to marry him would be it. If she'd meant what she'd said about not getting too serious, then she would turn him down flat. But if there was a part of her that felt even remotely like him, then she would at least consider it.

"Dad," Ian said, standing. "If this works, I'm going to owe you a lot more than a bonus check."

Ray smiled, toothy and worn. "Just learn from my mistakes, son."

The mere fact Ian was even considering something this drastic meant he already had.

• • •

By Thursday night, Pauly was exhausted. She'd celebrated with her family before they hit the road to return to Baltimore. She'd withdrawn her name from consideration for the Holymount position. She'd made arrangements with her landlord to keep her apartment until everything could be moved into storage. She'd participated in a conference call with members of the Cleveland Indians organization. And she'd broken the news to her team.

Because Ian had been oddly missing from equipment turn-in and bonus-check claim, she was extra anxious to see him. But, still, a part of her worried about how tonight would end and where that would leave them.

She wasn't good at long goodbyes.

Pauly flung her bat bag over her shoulder and picked up the other duffle bags packed with clothes and toiletries. At the bottom of the stairs, she backed through the metal door and exited into the parking lot. She always parked at the back of the lot, away from the idiots. Of course, some idiot always found her. Like now, when her shiny white car was eclipsed by a familiar-looking beast of a pickup truck.

Her hands tingled, and her limbs went loose.

Ian leaned against the grill of the truck. He wore a black T-shirt that stretched across his chest like it was made for him and blue jeans that looked as soft as a broken-in ball glove.

God, she loved him, and that was the only thing making this move difficult.

She shifted her gaze to the horizon before she started drooling or tearing up—or both. "Were you just going to stand there all night, hoping I came out?"

"No. When I pulled up, I saw your trunk was open. I figured you were packing, and I'm practicing my patience."

"Oh." *Odd.* Both the patience comment and the trunk. She looked down at the key fob in her hand. "I must've hit a button by accident."

She glanced at him, and he was smiling a sexy smile that made her want to either defend herself some more or jump him. Jumping him was definitely the stronger impulse.

"Can I help?" he asked.

Yes, you can go back to being the jerk you used to be, so I can leave without looking back. But she didn't want that, either.

"I'm good," she said, shaking her head. "This is all the stuff I'm taking right now."

While she tossed the bags in the trunk and closed the lid good and tight, Ian moved closer. Tucked between their cars, he looked nervous now. Almost jittery. Shoving his hands in and out of his front and back pockets and looking anywhere but at her.

"Missed you at the stadium today," she said.

That brought his attention back to her. Their eyes met, and she felt the sheer strength of their connection. Grainy images of everything they'd been through over the last several weeks flashed in her head. She'd been dead honest when she'd told him no matter where he was, she'd be pitching to him. He'd become a source of strength. A lot was about to change, but that never would.

"I went in early," Ian said. "To pick up my check."

"Mine's upstairs. I'll sign it over to you."

"No." He stepped closer, and she expected him to reach for her, but instead, he shoved his hands into his back pockets again. "I don't need the money anymore."

"But your dad?"

"All taken care of."

"How?"

"My Aunt May. And Ray. I've got to give him some credit, too. He's determined to do things differently." Ian's gaze intensified until it looked like he was staring right through her. "So am I."

"Ian—"

"Pauly." He went down on one knee, taking the air from her lungs. "I know this is going to seem crazy, but I love you." The unexpected words came out strong and clear, but they rattled her and mixed with other words: *What if he asks you to stay?* Like Tyler had, when he'd given her the ultimatum: baseball or him.

"You're only saying that because you don't want me to go," she said.

Ian frowned. "That's not it. Pauly, I love you. I want you to go, and I want to go with you. I would never dream of holding you back. Your dreams are my dreams. At least, I want them to be." He exhaled loudly. "I know words are just words, and I need to show you how serious I am, so ..." He pulled a ring from his back pocket and held it up between them.

She blinked back tears just to see his face.

"I want to be by your side on this incredible journey," he said. "I want to have your back when it gets rough. I want to be in your bed every night—when you're not on the road." He grinned, and the tension in her muscles released. "I know there are probably a million things we need to work out before you'll put this ring on your finger, but I need you to know how serious I am about you. About us. So I'm down here, asking you to marry me, even though I completely understand why it can't be right now." He tilted his head, a world of hope in his beautiful eyes. "What do you think?"

"I ..." Her heart pounded so loudly in her head, she couldn't keep her thoughts straight. "Is that what you did with your bonus check?"

"Yes." He gave a self-deprecating laugh and shook his head. "That was supposed to be your line, by the way."

Every common-sense brain cell told her not to jump in. *Sit with this. Think about it. Be rational. That's how you go places.* It took careful calculation and hard work to be a success. But she'd arrived here, in this moment, by taking a chance. One night, she just up and kissed her catcher in a Denny's parking lot. And she'd made her way to Cleveland in part by listening to that same guy tell her to pretend she was Big Unit. Which was ridiculous. And it was wonderful. And she wanted an entire life like that.

She smiled at the gorgeous man on the ground in front of her. "What is it about us and parking lots?"

"Right about now my knee's wishing we had a thing for grass."

"Oh, God." She rushed to him and pulled him to stand. "I love you, Ian. I do. And that"—she looked at the brilliant round solitaire winking up at her in the setting sun—"is so beautiful! I don't know how crazy things are going to be once I get to Cleveland, so I have no idea when we'll get to make it happen, but ..." She took a deep breath and jumped in. "Yes. I want to be with you."

He kissed her hard on the lips, infusing into that kiss just how worried he'd been, kneeling there, completely exposed, waiting for her to put him out of his misery. It made her realize just how much she didn't want to face this next phase of her life without him.

"I thought you were going to throw me out," he said, pulling back to look at her.

"Out of my apartment?" She offered her hand and watched him slide the ring onto her finger.

"No. Out of the game. I thought I'd hit a dinker to the pitcher and was running like mad to first, only to get thrown out in the end."

They admired the ring together for a minute, and then he raised her hand to his lips and kissed it.

"I don't think you hit a dinker at all, Pratt," Pauly said, stepping into him and lifting onto her toes. "I think you played the perfect game."

Acknowledgments

As much as I adore baseball, I couldn't have written this book in a believable way without input from the ball players in my life, especially my oldest son. Thank you, AJ, for answering my random texts about pitch counts and ball trajectory without making me feel silly for not knowing the answers after all these years.

I'm forever grateful to my editor, Tara Gelsomino, for her support and encouragement. Thanks as well to my copy editor, Annie Crosby, and Crimson Imprint Manager/Magician Julie Sturgeon. In fact, thank you to everyone at Simon & Schuster. I am honored to be a part of this amazing, dedicated team.

Finally, thank you to my family and friends, who never complain when I split my time between them and the characters in my head. You're the reason I can do what I do. I love you all. Madly.

About the Author

Elley Arden is a born-and-bred Pennsylvanian who has lived as far west as Utah and as far north as Wisconsin. She drinks wine like it's water (a slight exaggeration), prefers a night at the ballpark to a night on the town, and believes almond English toffee is the key to happiness. Elley writes books with charming characters, emotional stories, and sexy romance. For a complete list, visit www.elleyarden.com.

For more from Elley Arden, check out:

ARLINGTON ACES

The Change Up
The Sweet Spot
The Perfect Game

"Arden's unique voice and entertaining writing style really shine through in this unique romance." — Pure Jonel

"I liked how Helen Anne went from a timid mother and book-seller, to a strong woman who was not afraid to stand up for her-self." — Long and Short Reviews

CLEVELAND CLASH

Running Interference
Crossing Lines
Keeping Score

"Readers need not be sports fans to appreciate the strong female lead Arden has created in Tanya. Adding to the entertainment is the sweat-inducing physicality that occurs both on the field and off." – *Library Journal*

"Arden creates a heroine worthy of the MVP title … this sports romance [is] one to root for!" — Heroes and Heartbreakers

"I love the focus on women in sports, a very underappreciated and underexposed focal point for novels. The contrast between men's and women's pro football was quite poignant. Arden, writing with her usual well-polished, light-hearted style combines this all into an unforgettable package." — Pure Jonel

"I'm a sucker for second chance romances and *Running Interference* did not disappoint. This is my first Elley Arden read and I can guarantee it won't be my last. She has a unique writing style. Simple, yet strong with fluid and easy dialogue, you can't help but dive in and not come up until you're finished." — Eat Sleep Read Reviews

"I devoured the story ... Fun, sexy, and filled with smart ass side comments (and humor), this book is a great way to enter the world of the Cleveland Clash series." —4 stars, Art Books Coffee

THE KEMMONS BROTHERS baseball series

Save My Soul
Change My Mind
Heal My Heart
Take Me Out

"Nel and Gray have a lot of fun and challenging things to face . . . You will fall in love with them both . . . For a fun, sweet and very entertaining read, don't miss *Change My Mind* by Elley Arden." —Harlequin Junkie

"...Elley Arden really manages to evoke a barrage of emotions in her readers. She really has a way of creating novels that will touch you." —Texas Book Nook

"This is one of those novels that combines a multiplicity of different elements, backgrounds, and social stigmas into a single whole that will take your breath away and leave you reeling. Arden's

brilliant descriptions will paint a picture you won't soon forget."
—Pure Jonel

HARMONY FALLS

Crashing the Congressman's Wedding
Battling the Best Man
Marrying the Wrong Man

"The ending was my all-time favorite . . . This is definitely an AMAZING book that I recommend to all!" —Mamival's Books

"Good things come when you least expect it—at least I did with this book. I didn't expect to laugh, cry, and fall in love. But Elley Arden did those things to me, and after that short read, I think I'm coming back for more from this author." —Book Freak

EMERALD SPRINGS LEGACY

Chad's Chance

"The romance is hot and moves very quickly... deftly written and has a fun plot with the beer industry focus." —*InD'Tale Magazine*